The Realest IN THE GAME WANTS HER

A Novel By

TESHERA C.

© *2019 Royalty Publishing House*

Published by Royalty Publishing House
www.royaltypublishinghouse.com

ALL RIGHTS RESERVED
Any unauthorized reprint or use of the material is prohibited. No part of this book may be reproduced or transmitted in any form or by any means, electronic or mechanical, including photocopying, recording, or by any information storage without express permission by the author or publisher. This is an original work of fiction. Names, characters, places and incidents are either products of the author's imagination or are used fictitiously and any resemblance to actual persons, living or dead, is entirely coincidental.
Contains explicit language & adult themes suitable for ages 16+ only.

Royalty Publishing House is now accepting manuscripts from aspiring or experienced urban romance authors!

WHAT MAY PLACE YOU ABOVE THE REST:

Heroes who are the ultimate book bae: strong-willed, maybe a little rough around the edges but willing to risk it all for the woman he loves.

Heroines who are the ultimate match: the girl next door type, not perfect - has her faults but is still a decent person. One who is willing to risk it all for the man she loves.

The rest is up to you! Just be creative, think out of the box, keep it sexy and intriguing!

If you'd like to join the Royal family, send us the first 15K words (60 pages) of your completed manuscript to submissions@royaltypublishinghouse.com

Synopsis

> **I feel like the girl at the bar who's been there too much, can't stand up.**
>
> — ELLE VARNER

A wise person once said that the problem with revenge is that it never evens the score; it ties both the injured and the injurer to an escalator of pain. Both are stuck on the escalator as long as parity is demanded, and the escalator never stops.

Jahfar "Game" Gambino is the definition of humble and low-key. His main goal is to provide for his family while maintaining his lucrative career as a gaming creator. But even with his wealth and accomplishments, there is something that makes him toss and turn at night. Game has been going through his life harboring a hideous secret that could drive away the truest love that he has ever known.

Misty Blue lost her innocence at the tender age of eleven when she when was brutally attacked and witnessed the slaying of her mother. Abandoned by her father, the man who promised that he would never leave, Misty was then bounced around different foster homes. Unfortunately, her bad hand didn't stop there as she ended up succumbing to homelessness. Broken, empty, and simply tired of fighting, she meets the captivating Game. Although she has been let down by men all her life, she decides to take a chance on him hoping that she has outrun all of her bad days.

Once their two worlds collide, they endure the many emotions of the non-stop escalator called love, and neither of them are willing to get off. In this cat and mouse tale of crazy love, unspoken truths and unremedied rue, Misty and Game are forced to confront one another's pasts, learning that the old law about an eye for an eye almost always leaves everybody blind.

Misty Blue

"Bubble gum, bubble gum in the dish, how many pieces do you wish? One, two, three, four five," I sang along with my best friend in the whole world, Chandler. I was seriously out of breath, but I had to beat my jumping rope score that I had last week, which came in at six jumps, before I got too tired. Chandler had five, so at least I was beating her. The other girl who was turning one end of the rope wasn't as enthusiastic as we were about the game. She wasn't even singing along, and I guess it was because she could never get past three jumps because she was a little frumpy.

I finally got to seven jumps before collapsing on the ground, my curly pig-tails covering my face.

"Dang, I'm so tired y'all," I said to the two girls who were now sitting on the hot cement beside me.

"Maybe you're tired because you're always trying to show off," Tia said with a frown on her face.

"Girl, it's not my fault that your legs are too short and you always get tangled up in the rope." Chandler and I busted out laughing while Tia looked like she was mad as her beet-red face shined in the sun.

"You two girls stop picking on Tia and come in here from out of that sun," my mom chastised. "It's 100 degrees out here and y'all are the only three girls outside sweating your behinds off."

"Yes Mommy," I replied before getting up from the driveway and running towards the door. My mom was right; it was hot as heck outside and officially the first week of summer break. The next school year I would be heading to junior high school, so I planned to have lots of fun this summer before the new school year started.

The girls and I piled up one-by-one at the kitchen island, and my mom had all the fixings for ice cream sundaes. There was chocolate syrup, cookies, M&M's, gummy bears, and more. We were in sundae heaven.

"Girls, I wanted to let you all know how good you did during the school year and that I'm so excited that you will be going to junior high next year. So, eat up, and you all better not be out here fussing, or I won't do this again. We all nodded simultaneously as I piled gummy bears on my ice cream and dug in.

"So, do y'all think that boy Jeremy who came to our school late is cute?" Tia quizzed as she scooped cookies on her ice cream.

"He's okay. But why does he wear that rusty old hat all of the time?" I asked.

"I don't know but he asked me to be his girlfriend," Tia said innocently.

"Girl, he only likes you because you're light skin." Chandler rolled her eyes.

"Sooooo!" Tia yelled childishly. Tia and Chandler always went back and forth over anything under the sun, and today it was skin color. While Tia had a yellowish hue to her, Chandler resembled the chocolate ice cream that we were eating. And me, well I was right in the middle with a toned, bronze complexion.

"Y'all better chill out before my mom comes back. It doesn't matter what color we are, we are all cute." I flipped my hair.

"Well anyway, I'm going to tell him I will go steady with him."

"Go steady with who?" I heard a voice enter the kitchen and beamed when I turned around to see my father. I hopped off the stool and jumped into his arms. I was like an ant in his arms. He was so big that his entire frame swallowed me.

"Hi Daddy. How was summer school?" I asked, kissing his cheek.

"School was school sweetheart." He smiled and then sat me back on the stool.

"Hey girls," he said, acknowledging Tia and Chandler.

"Hi Mr. Blue!" they both yelled simultaneously. My dad was a middle school teacher and unfortunately, he was stuck with teaching summer school, which ruined all my plans. I had planned for us to go to the beach every day, but now I had to wait for him to come home and nap or something like that.

"Misty," he called out to me while snooping in the fridge. "Did you get your reading done today baby girl?"

"Yes Daddy," I replied. "I read two chapters of *Charlotte's Web*."

"Good. You know once you're done, you will have a book report, right? So, make sure that you are not just speeding through just so that you can finish."

"Okay Daddy," I said, staring up at him. My daddy was the best in my eyes. He tucked me into bed every night, helped me with stuff, bought me anything that I wanted, and he gave me these big bear hugs that made me squeal every time. He was originally from Haiti. He came here when he was eighteen with nothing but $500 and a dream. He landed a kiss on my forehead before jogging up the steps.

"Your daddy is so nice Misty. He always gives us dollars and he got y'all this big tail house," Tia chimed.

"I know girl. That is my daddy!" I said before we finished the rest of our ice cream and went back outside to play.

Game Gambino

"Girl, shut up, with yo' big ole five head."

"No, you shut up before I tell everybody that you still pee in the bed, with your pissy ass," Kayla screamed so loud that the entire neighborhood probably heard it through our cracked window. I walked up to her slowly with my fist balled the entire time. I was going to show her who was pissy.

"Boy, you better not," I heard my older sister, Danni, yell from the doorway. "Mama gone kick your ass if you don't get down there and wash them dishes before she gets home. And why are you walking around here in your drawers?"

"Man, Jalen is hogging the room and I can't get in there." The next thing I knew, Danni was banging on the room door that I shared with my older brother.

"Jalen, if you got some nasty girl in there you gone get it because I'm snitching." It was apparent that he did have someone in there because she was making weird moaning sounds. Those were usually the sounds that girls made every time my older brother Jalen took them in our room.

"Keyshia, if you are in there, my mama will be home in thirty minutes!" Danni yelled with a mischievous grin on her face.

"Who the fuck is Keyshia?" we heard the girl yelling from the other side of the door.

The only thing I could do was laugh because Danni knew that Keyshia wasn't in that room. Only God knew who it was the way my brother moved. He was that nigga in the hood and girls flocked to him.

Some girl stormed out of the room buttoning her shirt.

"You ain't shit, Jalen," she continued to yell before storming down the brick stairs so hard that I thought her feet would break. The Park steps were no joke and you could lose your life fucking with them.

"Damn Danni, why you such a hater?" Jalen laughed as if the whole situation was comical to him.

"You's a dirty dog," Danni said while mushing him in the face. "Now go and find a shirt, lil' boy, so that you can wash those damn dishes," Danni turn to me and ordered.

I didn't get why she thought that she was the boss of everyone. Jalen was the oldest, then her, then me, and last was Kayla. She and I were only nine months apart from each other, so everyone called us twins. Danni was only two years older than me, so I didn't get why she thought that she could boss me around. She would get enough of that shit eventually, though.

I found a shirt and sighed while looking at the stack of dirty dishes. It would take me forever to finish them, so I wouldn't even be able to go outside and catch up with my friends. Just then I heard the sound of the front screen door creek.

"Why in the world do y'all have my door open letting all of the air out?" I heard my mother fuss.

I hurried to her side and helped her with her bags. She smiled before pecking me on the head.

"Baby, where is everybody?" she asked, finally sitting down and removing her slip-resistant shoes.

"They're upstairs," I answered plainly.

"And why do you have that look on your face son? You look like you just lost your best friend. I know you want to go outside, so gone 'head, but you better be back in this house before the streetlights come on Jahfar Gambino."

"Dang Ma, I'm twelve years old. I should be able to stay out 'til at least 9 pm," I complained.

"Or you could just not go outside since you like to complain." I took the hint and grabbed my game boy and dashed out of the door.

"MAMA!" I heard Danni yell from the steps. "He didn't even wash those dishes!"

"How about you come down here and wash them since you like telling on everybody!" Mom yelled.

I laughed at Danni's snitching ass finally getting what was coming to her.

"Yoooooo Game," I heard my name being called from the green box. I walked over to where it was and dapped up my cousin, Rod, who stayed three courts away from me. His mama and my mama were sisters and applied for a park house at the same time and got them. The Park was what some people called the hood. It consisted of low-income housing and plenty of drama. Youngs Terrace projects was known as one of the most dangerous parks in Norfolk and it was where I called my home.

I walked past the neighborhood crackhead, Smitty, as he smiled a toothless smile.

"What's up Smitty?" I greeted him while dapping him up.

"What's up youngin'? You got a dollar for me?" I dug in my pocket and all I had was fifty cents, so I passed it to him.

"This is all I got," I said, handing it to him.

"Thanks man. You're alright! You're one of the good ones. I don't know about your cousin over there," he said, pointing to Rod.

"Make sure you watch yourself and watch him too," he said as he limped away from me in search of his next hit.

"Why are you over there talking to that fool?" Rod asked once I finally reached him.

"Man, Smitty don't bother nobody."

"He's a crackhead, and we got plenty of them in our family to know how they operate." Rod was right, and his dad happened to be one of them as well. He would steal the shirt off your back if you would let him, so that he could get high.

"Man anyway, what's up? I heard you have to go to summer school. Is Mr. Blue your teacher?"

"Nope. I was mad as hell they didn't put me in his class," Rod replied.

"Well dude, you should've gone to class in the first place and you wouldn't even be in summer school." I chuckled. Rod was repeating the seventh grade for the third time and he didn't seem to care one bit.

"Boy, shut up." He shoved me causing my Gameboy to fall out of my hands.

"Damn dog! Quit playing so much," I fussed while picking my Gameboy up and wiping the dirt off it."

"Nigga stop crying. Ain't nobody tell you to bring that thing out anyway. You take that shit everywhere like you slow."

"You just mad because you don't have one. I can take it everywhere with me if I want and you ain't gone do nothing about it!" I was upset with Rod for trying to carry me. I guess he was right though, my Gameboy was my life; any type of game for that matter. That's where I got my name from; my love of this one game.

Just then, I heard a commotion coming from the middle of the park. We stayed in the back, but not too far back that we couldn't hear when some drama was about to pop off. Rod and I both ran towards it and there was a group of people standing around two girls who looked like they were about to fight. As I got closer, I noticed that it was the girl who was in my house earlier with my brother. The other girl was this lil' skinny, light-skinned girl named Keyshia. She was supposed to be my brother's girlfriend and she was from Oak Leaf Park, also known as the suburbs of the hoods.

"Bitch, someone told me that they saw you coming from my man's house, so what's up?" Keyshia yelled over the ruckus.

"Girl, I didn't even know he was your boyfriend, but I did let him eat my coochie though!" the other girl called out.

"Bitch, you a hoe!" was the last thing said before Keyshia stole off on ole girl. The two of them began tussling before Keyshia's friend, Big Gabby, jumped in the fight. Now Gabby was three times the size of the average person. I would compare her size to Barney. Gabby slung the poor girl so hard that it looked like she flew over me.

"Yeah bitch, now what!" Keyshia said to the girl as she was curled up in the fetal position.

"Stay the fuck away from Jalen, bitch!" With that, she kicked the girl so hard in her ribs that I for sure heard them crack.

Jalen was nowhere to be found while all of this was going on, and he was the cause of all the commotion. I guess this was just ratchet activity, and today was just another day in the hood.

Misty Blue

I waited by the door patiently, as my dad would be home any minute now. I wanted to tell him that I had finished *Charlotte's Web*. Every time I finished a novel, my dad would buy me a crystal to add to my collection. I loved crystals and had a book full of them. So far, I had fourteen. My daddy finally pulled up in his big, shiny Lincoln, which he called his baby.

"Misty, would you go upstairs and get Mommy's medication?" I heard my mom ask but ignored her. Her hand landing on my behind knocked me out of my trance.

"Mommy! I'm waiting for Daddy," I whined.

"Misty Annabelle Blue, your dad will still be here when you get back. Now get!" She snapped her fingers. I raced to get the medication which she took every day in the afternoon. She told me she had to take medication because she had a big heart, so I just went with it. By the time I made it back down the stairs, I noticed that my mother and father were in some sort of heated whispering match.

"Brock, we didn't discuss this. How well do you know them?" I heard.

"Mina, I've taught these boys for two years. They are good kids, they're just in bad situations."

"Okay, and you couldn't have taken them out somewhere? You had to bring them to our home where your daughter and I lay our heads?"

"Come on Mina, you're making too much out of this. Don't forget that you and I came from places similar to where they have."

I guessed that stumped Mommy because after that, a small smile appeared on her face

"Well, bring them in. I know you weren't going to keep them in the car all this time." My father kissed my mom, then disappeared outside, and I wondered what was going on.

My father came back a few seconds later with two boys following behind him. They looked like they were my age, but that was the only commonality we shared. These boys looked rough; way different from the people who attended my Christian private school. The tall one who was so black that he was purple stared mischievously while his shoes folded at the top. The janks started talking to me way before he did. The boy next to him was short but didn't look as mean. I spotted two holes in his pants along with his t-shirt that was two sizes too big. The three of us just stood there staring.

"Misty, are you going to just stand there? Say hi to our guests. This is Larod and Jahfar. Guys, this is my baby, Misty. I hid behind my father's legs because these boys were scary, especially the one named Larod. The look in his eyes wasn't a good one.

"Misty? What type of name is that?" Larod said before laughing, and Jahfar joined him.

"It's my name! That's what it is, with your big head. What have you been cutting your hair with? A weed whacker?" I asked, stepping aside so that he could see me.

"And what are you laughing at, JAHFAR? You may as well cut those pants into shorts because they are just about to reach your knees already.

"Whatever lil' girl, and my name is Game!"

"Alright! Y'all have plenty of time to argue. How about lunch?" my dad intervened.

We followed him into the kitchen and in the nick of time, Chandler and Tia were walking through the back door.

"Hey peeps!" Chandler announced as she walked in and made herself comfortable at the table.

"You better peep your butt and wash your hands," my mom said to both Tia and Chandler.

They did as they were told and then sat back down. Chandler kept sneaking looks at Larod while Tia paid neither one of them any attention. She and Jeremy had made it official a week ago, so all she could think about was him. My mom sat a platter of grilled cheese sandwiches, tomato soup and fruit in front of us.

"You all dig in and have as much as you want boys. I will be in the family room. Be good," my mom said to all of us but maintained eye contact with me before she moseyed off.

We sat at the table for a good five minutes before I finally spoke up.

"So why do they call you Game, JAHFARRRR," I said, stretching out his name and making Tia and Chandler laugh.

"Because I like to play games. Why do you think, dumb?"

"Boy, you're dumb! Don't call my friend dumb," Tia chimed in.

"Girl, mind your business," Rod said to her.

"You mind yours, with your greedy self. Do you eat at home? You done had three sandwiches already!" Chandler retorted.

"Come on y'all! Let's go," I said. "We can leave these fat boys in here." We burst out in a fit of laughter as we each skipped out of the kitchen.

"What do y'all want to do today? I'm tired of playing jump rope all the time," Chandler said, throwing the jump rope down to the ground.

"Let's go to the park or something," Tia suggested.

"Okay cool," I said as I put my rope and chalk on the porch. Just as we were walking, the back door opened.

"We're going too," Larod said with a smile before wrapping his arm around Tia.

"Ewww, if you don't get off of me," Tia said, and then we skipped away leaving the boys behind. The park was packed and I immediately spotted Jeremy and his boys, Stephen and Chris. Tia was so busy swinging that she didn't even notice him.

"Bet you can't push me high," I said to Game, and he took that as a challenge. Silly boy. I knew he could push me high. I said that to trick him. He pushed for a few minutes before he stopped.

"Aite girl. My arms are tired now."

"Well thanks," I replied, and what do you know, he actually smiled. This was a major difference from the mean mug that he had been wearing all day.

"Who are these boys?" I heard Jeremy say from behind me. He and his friends had walked over and now he was talking to Tia.

"I saw you walk in with them. You and I go together, so why are you chilling with other boys?"

"Jeremy, we all can hang out together. Dang!" she said.

"I don't know these dirty boys. Why would I want to hang with them?"

That got Game's attention.

"What did you just say boy?" Game spoke up.

"Did I stutter?" Jeremy replied.

"Man, I'm not even stunting you," Game said, and then attempted to walk away.

"Come over here with us," Jeremy said to Tia while grabbing her arm.

"No Jeremy," she said, trying to pull away from him. The next thing I saw was Jeremy falling to the ground after Game punched his lights out.

"What is your problem boy? I don't even have a daddy and I have sense enough to know to never grab on a girl. Carry yo' punk ass home, and I better not see you in this park again!" Game said, making Jeremy and his friends scatter like roaches.

"Dang JAHFARRRRR! I thought you didn't like us," I said, amazed by the way he had just stood up for Tia.

"I don't, but Mr. Blue is my dog and you're his daughter, so that counts for something." He then walked away and joined Larod, who was now macking on some girl. I watched him walk away and I couldn't help but think that I was actually starting to like him.

Game Gambino

It was another blazing day in the hood and everyone and their mama was outside hustling, gossiping, and scheming. I walked past the local dope boys as they were shooting dice on the corner. Each one of them niggas was fly, rocking Christen Dior and some more shit. I wondered how a small piece of rock could have niggas fresh to death like they were. I found myself dreaming of the day when I could dress like them, spit game to girls like them, and most of all, get money like them.

I walked down the street with no destination in sight, thinking about the bullshit that Rod had just sprung on me. He was forever scheming and now wanted me to get down with some shit that he was trying to do. I wasn't with scheming, especially from people that tried to help us. I knew the moment that Mr. Blue took us to his house, Rod's wheels would start turning, and sure enough, he had come up with this plan for us to rob them.

Too bad he would have to do it himself because I wouldn't fuck Mr. Blue and his family over, not after they welcomed me into their home and treated me nice. That was the difference between my cousin and I. I was living to survive while he was living to die. There had been a series of break-ins in the neighborhood and no one knew that it was Rod. Now he thought that he'd hit the jackpot going to Mr. Blue's house. Hopefully he wouldn't get caught up, but maybe that was what he needed to calm his ass down.

I finally made my way home and it was quiet, surprisingly. The snitch, Danni, was out with her friends, Kayla and my mom were sleeping, and who knew where Jaylen was or who he was doing. I settled on the couch and pulled out my Gameboy, and no more than five minutes into me playing, the door was opened abruptly, and in walked my brother with Keyshia right on his heels yelling up a storm.

"I don't care what you say Jaylen, I am keeping this baby," she yelled.

"Man, I don't give a fuck. That don't mean I'ma take care of it!"

"Grow up and be a man Jaylen! I didn't lay down and have sex with myself."

It's like they didn't even see me sitting on the couch as they continued to go back and forth, finally waking up my mother.

"What the hell is going on down here?" she asked, as she tied her housecoat tighter. The two of them suddenly became quiet and I noticed the puffy circles around my mother's eyes. I could tell she had been crying.

"Mama, what's wrong?" I asked, with a hint of concern in my voice.

"Nothing baby, Mama is fine. Now what is going on down here? And what was all that yelling about?"

"Well Ms. Evelyn, I'm pregnant, and the baby is Jaylen's."

Silence

Mama shut her eyes tight as she dropped her head.

"Mama we gone get a test. We don't even know if it's mine."

"Shut up Jaylen. I don't want to hear nothing from you right now. I couldn't stop you from having sex, so I made sure that you had condoms so that this wouldn't happen, and now look. How are we supposed to bring another mouth in here to feed? Huh? I just got laid off from cleaning the hospital, so what are we supposed to do now?" she cried out.

"Mama..." my brother started, but she only silenced him with the wave of her hand. Her once golden skin was now Casper white as she looked like the wind had been knocked out of her. Times like this, I wondered where my bitch ass daddy was. Mama couldn't teach boys to be men and she had to do it all by herself. I guess he just upped and decided that he didn't want to be a father anymore and bounced. I was thirteen years old and I hadn't seen my daddy since I was four years old. I barely even remember the nigga, but if he couldn't be a man for Mama, I would, and I now knew what I had to do. I called up Rod and let him know that I was down with whatever he wanted to do.

Rod decided that we would hit the Blue's house that night, and though I didn't want to do it, I had to. The closer we got to their home, the more the butterflies erupted in my stomach.

"Look nigga, you have to get rid of that scary shit. I already told you that we're good. The last time that we were there I left the window up in the downstairs bathroom, so all we have to do is slip through it. I also watched him put his code into his safe in his office, so we're good as gold. We should be in and out in five minutes or less. I really need you to come through for me cousin," he prepped me.

"Alright, I'm down. Let's just hurry up and get this shit over with."

We caught the bus over town and then walked the rest of the way to their house. It was twelve in the morning and we waited around the back of the house making sure that everyone was sleeping. I took one last breath before it was time to start the show. It was now or never.

Misty Blue

I knew I should've listened to Daddy when he told me about drinking after 9 pm. I tried to hold my pee for as long as I could because I did not want to get out of my comfy bed, but my bladder was not having it. Walking like a zombie with my eyes still closed, I made it to the bathroom to relieve myself. It felt so good, as I'd had one too many cups of pop tonight. After finishing, I washed my hands and could have sworn I heard something down the stairs. I shut the water off for a moment, but only quietness loomed around me.

Once I was finished wiping my hands, I wobbled back to my bed and as soon as my head hit the pillow I was out. I didn't know how much time had passed, but I felt a little saliva hit my hand and as I was turning over to get more comfortable, I heard a loud thud. This time I knew that my ears were not failing me, so I slowly crept out of bed and headed downstairs. Not one to be afraid of much, I decided to go and take a look. It probably was just my mother anyway; she always crept around when we were sleeping. By the time I made it halfway down the staircase, I heard the sound of voices and a whimper. I peeked my head over the balcony and what I saw almost made me scream out.

There my mother was, laid out on the ground tied up. I could see blood

THE REALEST IN THE GAME WANTS HER

spilling from her head while the light in my dad's study was on. I hurriedly ran back up to my room to use my bedroom telephone to call the police, but the phone line was dead.

"Shit!" I cursed. I had never in my eleven years said a curse word, and up until now, I never had the desire to. Unsure of what to do, I went to hide under my bed, hoping that the bad people would just get what they'd come for and go away. I laid still under my bed as I heard the sound of footsteps approaching. I so wished that tonight wouldn't have been the night that Dad chose to hang out with his friends. Out of all the nights.

"Yo, where she at?" I heard the familiar voice say, but I couldn't quite place it, too scared that the person would hear me thinking.

"I don't know man. We got what we came for, so let's just go," another voice said.

There was a brief silence and before I knew it, I was being pulled out from under the bed by my feet. My nightgown flew up and my barely there boobs were on display. There stood two masked boys, but their piercing stare made a chill run through my spine. The tears immediately began to fall from my eyes as I called out for my daddy.

"Your pops can't save you now Misty." The way he said my name made me feel so familiar with him, but I still couldn't place him.

The next thing he did was unexpected. He tugged at my princess panties before he eventually pulled them off. I tried to fight him off, but he was too strong.

"Please. No," I cried.

"Man, what are you doing? This was not a part of the plan," the other one said, trying to pull him off me.

The mean one only ignored him as he did the unthinkable and rammed himself inside of me.

"Ohhh, DADDDDYYYY MOMMMMY! HELP ME!" The pain that

19

shot through me was something that I had never felt. He moved in and out of me, grunting, with sweat pouring from his forehead.

The other boy stood there with his shoulders slumped like he wanted to protest, but he didn't. The torture lasted for longer than I could count, and when it was over, he rested on top of me trying to catch his breath. He then hopped up and began to dress. I stared into his eyes trying to figure out why he had done this to me. But I had to turn away because there was an evil in his eyes that overpowered me. The masked boys then left my room and disappeared. Just as quickly as they had ruined my life, they were gone.

Misty Blue

Present

14 years later

I hated the cold. I hated it so much that when I was a little girl, I refused to go outside in the winter. My friends would knock at my door and throw rocks at my window for me to come down and play, but I only ignored them. I would have much rather been cuddled up next to my dad while he graded papers and I drank my hot chocolate with extra marshmallows.

Today was much like those bitter, cold days that I hated. A light coat of snow covered the ground and the wind that swept across my face was like the worst punishment that I had ever endured. People huddled up close to their families as they scurried in and out of the busy shopping centers and restaurants. Thanksgiving had just passed and now people were in the holiday spirt as they spent endless amounts of money on their kinfolk. It was 8:00 pm and the streets were still packed being that the malls and shops stayed open later because of the holidays.

I stood unnoticed as people whizzed by me; their smiles repulsing and their laughter obnoxious. So many people being in the holiday spirit made it impossible for me to relax. I couldn't wait until the streets were clear and quiet so that I could get back to my life. The next two hours were filled with people walking to and from and breaking the bank for material shit before it finally calmed down. Finally, I could rest. My feet were eating through my shoes from walking all day, and on top of that, I was freezing in the 30-degree weather.

I removed my knapsack from my back and took out a little quilt that my grandmother had sent me from Hatti so many years ago that I couldn't remember. I kept it close to me just so that I could feel a little closer to my family. Next, I fetched a piece of cardboard from the trash and laid the quilt on top of it. I placed my knapsack down and balled it up a little so that it resembled somewhat of a pillow. I laid down on the blanket and cardboards and wrapped the remaining little of the quilt around my body. It didn't take much seeing that I was a pretty frail woman. The quilt gave me little warmth, but it wasn't much against the harsh weather. Dripples of snow flowed above me, finally connecting with my face and dancing with my tears. I didn't even know that I was crying or what I was even crying for.

It was my fault that I was the way that I was. Many theories, such as the Adlerian and the Existential theory, stressed the importance of all people having choices in life, and me, well I guess I had just made the wrong choices. My incessant crying had finally put me to sleep, but it was short lived as I was awakened to a flashlight being shined in my face.

"Ma'am, this is private property. You can't sleep here," the heavy black lady said.

I wiped the sleep out of my eyes and realized that she was a cop, and I instantly froze up. There had been too many instances with black people and the police, and they all ended the same way; a black person ending up at the morgue.

"Excuse me ma'am! Did you hear me? Get up right now! You cannot be here."

I quickly grabbed my bearings, which was pretty much nothing, and stood to my feet.

"If I catch you here again, I will write you a citation. It's so many shelters, why don't you go find one?" she said rudely. The snow had finally stopped, but there was still about three inches covering the ground and ice everywhere. I took my time so that I wouldn't slip as I carried my bag and cardboard.

"You need to hurry up!" the lady yelled. "I'm not going to feel bad for you because you are homeless. We all get the same twenty-four hours in a day and you chose to waste yours."

"I don't have anywhere to go," I finally said, my voice cracking.

"Not my problem!" she answered before she finally got back into her police car, leaving me walking with no destination in sight.

Game Gambino

I enjoyed the quietness of my home. It was the space that I most cherished. There was no music, no TV, no one asking me for anything, no nothing. Just quiet, the way I liked it. I worked best when I was free of distraction and in my own element. My mind had a funny way of working. At 3:00 in the morning, while the rest of the world was sleeping, my wheels would burn my brain forcing me to wake up. That was usually when I got the most work done.

It was now 8 am and I was sitting in the same spot that I had been in for the last four hours. I had been spending my days and nights working on creating a new game that recognized autism awareness. Yes, I had turned my love for gaming into a career and I wanted to do something different, so here I was. I closed my MacBook Air and decided that was enough for now. I didn't want to end up getting burnt out and not being able to finish the project, or Microsoft would kick my ass.

I stepped into the scalding hot shower as the jets rained down on me. The water soothed me and the sound of it crashing down took me to another place. A place where all my past sins were washed away and I was given ultimate forgiveness for anyone that I had ever hurt. I handled my business for another fifteen minutes before getting out and preparing for the day. I worked from home mostly; however, I checked in to the office on a weekly basis for staff and interest meetings. But for the most part, I was my own boss. Today I was going to meet my boy to shoot some hoops and check on my mom and sister.

I slipped on some balling shorts, a t-shirt, and sneakers and got ready to meet up with my shit-talking homeboy. He loved coming with all that rah shit and then ended up getting his ass smoked on the court. I put some baby spinach, banana, almond milk, yogurt and bee pollen into the blender so that I could have my daily breakfast. To practice discipline and growth, I was doing a fast where I didn't eat until sunset, so this smoothie would hold me over until then.

I heard the sound of my door opening, so I knew it must've been someone who had a key, which was only a handful of people. I didn't even bother checking because I heard the person before they even got to me.

"BROTHHHHERRRR, where you at?" I heard my older sister, Danni, yell. She was always coming to my house without an invitation being ratchet and shit. She literally yelled until she finally heard the blender going in the kitchen. I just looked at her.

"What did I tell you about that? Don't come into my house causing all of that discord, yelling and shit," I said calmly while looking at her like she was simple.

"Whatever Jahfar! I was just in the neighborhood and decided to stop by," she said, going into my fridge.

"You're always in the area I see. Tell me this, you live thirty minutes away from me, so how is it that you are always in the area?" I said, more like a statement than an actual question, but she only ignored me.

"You need to go shopping. You don't have anything in this fridge boy!"

"I'm fasting. And when I'm not, I'm not filling my body with all that swine that you like. You're looking a little unhealthy anyway, so you might want to get it together," I joked.

"Boy, you want to be a white person so bad, don't you?" she joked.

"Gone head with all of that mess. I'm a black man with two black daughters. Why would I want to be anything other than what I'm destined to be? Watch your mouth," I said seriously.

"Okay, lil' dirty. I didn't mean to get you upset. I know you're all about protecting your energy, so my bad."

"Yeah, respect my energy too. What's Mama been doing? You still staying there, right?" I joked.

"Man, hell yeah, and she's been churching me to death. She and her husband. I got to find me another place ASA,P or I'm just going to go back home to Mario."

"Well you know I'm here if you need help with anything. If I got it, you got it."

Even though Danni was my big sister, I tended to act the oldest, getting her out of shit and helping her out when I could.

"I know bruh, but you have helped enough. I got to do something on my own, but thank you."

That was just like Danni and me. We were arguing one minute and loving on each other the next. My mom had raised us to be close, so we lived by the principle that family came first.

"Well, I'm about to get out of here. Lock up when you leave and don't fuck up my shit," I teased her but was serious as hell. On the way out, I noticed that my picture of Nipsey Hussle was a little crooked, so I fixed it. I would call myself obsessive compulsive, but I liked shit how I liked it. I grabbed my gym bag and made my way outside. I was a damn fool to had come out with some damn shorts on, but I would definitely warm up when I got to my location. I was bobbing my head

THE REALEST IN THE GAME WANTS HER

to Nipsey's *Victory Lap* album as it blared through my speakers when I felt my phone vibrate in my pocket.

"Hello," I answered.

"Ohhh, so I see that I have to call you from a different number so you can answer, Game. That's messed up."

"What's up Ko? You called me to complain? Or do you have some real shit to say?"

"Yesses, I miss you daddy," she whined into the phone. That was my biggest turn off with some females. And Ko needed to grow the fuck up and realize that her being fine as wine with a nice ass didn't move me when her head was empty.

"Yo, don't call me Daddy. I'm not that nigga that fucked you up in the head, and you're not my kid."

"Well damn. I guess we just gon' say fuck all the pleasantries, so why don't you come through."

I shook my head at Ko's frankness, but it wasn't unexpected. This had been her attitude since I rescued her off the streets two years ago, and it was also her biggest downfall. She didn't give a fuck about anything, and that shit was unattractive to say the least. But that didn't mean that I wasn't a man with needs.

"I will see you tonight Ko, and don't keep me waiting. If you're not home, I'm leaving."

"Okay. I will see you later," she said seductively, and I could've sworn my dick jumped.

I hadn't been in a relationship for two years, and honestly didn't want to. Over time, a few women had occupied my time, but KoKo was the one that I just couldn't seem to stay away from. I didn't know if it was her head that she blessed me with daily, or if it was the need for me to fix broken people. It seemed like those were the women that I was

TESHERA C.

most attracted to. I called them fixer uppers; even my kids' mom. When I first met her as a teen, she'd come from a broken home where her dad was an alcoholic and used to beat the shit out of her and her mom. I headed to the indoor court making a mental note to add Ko to my to-do list, literally.

Misty Blue

The morning had come too soon, but the good thing about it was the sun offered a little heat. I got up and grabbed my things before walking to a nearby McDonald's. When I got there, I quickly disappeared into the restroom and used it as a wash area. I used paper towels to wash my delicate parts with water and I used the hand soap to wash under my armpits. I took a swig out of the travel sized mouthwash that I had stolen from the store a few weeks back and used it to gargle before fixing my shaggy clothes and walking out. McDonald's was a little busy as the lunch crowd had just piled in.

"Order thirty-four," I heard the man behind the counter say, and a man walked up and grabbed his order. Right after that he yelled, "Order 42!" He shouted it out two times and no one had come forward to claim the meal, so the worker sat the food on the counter. Once he walked back to the back, I slowly headed to the exit, but not before quickly snatching the bag and making a dash for it.

"Hey! Come back here burger thief," I heard someone say, but I was running like I was a track star.

I finally stopped running when I made it back to my new living space.

It was on the side alley near a host of clothing and food shops. I sat on my cardboard and took out the food in the bag. It was a quarter pounder, large fry and two baked apple pies. I hated quarter pounders, but I was about to tear it up. A hot meal beat digging in the trash for people's leftovers. Once I finished, I was stuffed, but I knew that the fullness in my tummy would dissipate any minute now. That's how it was after I ate after not eating for a while; something would fill me for a few minutes and then I would be starving again.

I pulled out a piece of paper from my knapsack. It was a Friday's application that I had gotten two weeks ago. It was halfway filled out, so I decided to finish it. I sat it down while I searched for a pen and it flew away.

"Shit!" I cursed before running after it. The wind was blowing hard as hell, as every time I got a hold on it, it flew in another direction. I was so determined to get it that I smashed dead into someone.

"Damn yo," I heard a voice say. "You're scuffing up my Timbs bitch." I had fallen slam dead into him and fell on my bottom. I looked up to see a pretty decent looking man, but the scowl that he wore on his face scared the life out of me. It reminded me of my third foster dad.

"Yo, are you slow? Get up!" he demanded.

"I'm so sorrryyy," I stuttered while trying to get up from the wet snow.

"Yo, chill man. Can't you see she just fell? You could've helped her up or something," another man said from behind him. He pushed him away and then helped me up.

"You good?" he asked. I only shook my head up and down, afraid of opening my mouth so I wouldn't piss him off like I had just done his friend.

"You sure? You need to sit down or something? This is my sister's spot," he said, pointing to the Juice Bar that was right next to my temporary home.

"You can go and sit down if you need to."

"I'm okay," I lowly replied, knowing that I wasn't. It felt like I had busted my damn knee and I didn't even get the application back.

"Alright, I'ma take your word for it, but don't ever let nobody disrespect you. Demand that shit! And I apologize on behalf of my friend. Take care," he said and then walked into the Juice Bar. His friend only smirked and walked behind him.

I went back to my space and thought about what the kind man had just said to me. He was totally different from his friend, so I didn't get why they were even together. But I couldn't focus on that. I pulled out a newspaper and looked in the wanted ads for jobs, when I heard laughter from the mean man and his friend. His friend walked ahead of him and he glanced back to where I was, and for a brief moment, it looked like he could see right through me. I turned my head quickly out of embarrassment. When I looked back, he was gone and I got on with the rest of my day.

Game Gambino

I pulled up to KoKo's crib ready to hear some bullshit that I knew she would be talking. She loved telling me about things that I particularly didn't care about. There were a lot of things that I disliked about Ko, but one thing that I loved for sure, was that she didn't want a relationship. Yeah, she could get a little clingy, but we were on the same page when it came to the relationship shit. As long as she wasn't around here fucking tons of niggas and was respecting herself, I was cool.

I walked into her place and she was dressed in her birthday suit as usual. She walked around clapping her ass and smoking a blunt, another thing I didn't like.

"Yo, put that shit out!" I demanded.

"What nigga? You got asthma or something?"

I could tell her goofy ass was high as a rocket, but she put it out and plopped all that ass on me. I grabbed a handful of it.

"Doesn't addiction run in your family? Why the hell you keep smoking?"

THE REALEST IN THE GAME WANTS HER

"Game, it's just weed." She pouted.

"Yep, and that's how it always starts off."

I wasn't dating Ko or anything, but I did care about her, which was the main reason I pulled her from prostituting and got her a spot. I couldn't keep trying to guilt her into not smoking. Everyone had their vices.

"You hate smoking but let me show you what I can do."

She stroked my dick alive through the sweats that I was wearing as I laid back and enjoyed the show. The next thing she did was light her blunt back up and started to blow smoke rings out of her mouth. She pulled my dick out and by now, it was rock solid. The smoke rings then landed around my dick while Ko held a little smoke in her mouth. She then put her pretty little mouth around my dick and went for what she knew. I didn't know what it was, but the mixture of the warmth of the smoke and her deep throating my whole dick had my toes curled like a bitch.

Her slurping and gagging on my dick was like music to my ears as I palmed her bald head. Ko was going for that 90's Jada Pinkett look, but she definitely wasn't sucking dick like Jada. She was sucking it like a female who needed her phone bill paid. I yanked away from her, but she only swallowed my dick again. I didn't want to cum in her mouth, but baby girl was giving me no option.

"I can take it!" she said with her mouth still around me, but I understood her perfectly. No sooner than she said it, I exploded in her mouth and she didn't even flinch. She drank it like it was her favorite drink, not missing a drop. She looked at me with those doe eyes. "Baby, I want you to fuck me."

She didn't have to tell me what she knew I was going to do. I yanked her up and she laid on the leather sectional with her ass up, begging me to fuck her. I entered her hard and strong just like she liked it, and she screamed to the top of her lungs. "AHHHHH SHIT! Do that shit nigga!" She started talking her usual shit as I plunged in and out of her with my thumb in her butt.

"Throw that shit back Ko!" I demanded, and she appeased my request. Ko was wet as hell, leaking actually. Her juices covered my dick making a slapping sound each time I went in and out of her. It didn't take too much longer for me to bust all over her ass. Ko would never catch me slipping busting in her no matter how good the shit felt.

Ko drifted off to sleep like a baby and the minute she closed her eyes, I slipped out. I had never slept at Ko's house and I was not about to start. I got home, showered and laid in my bed while some bullshit was playing on the TV that I paid absolutely no attention to. Out of nowhere, the girl from earlier popped in my head; the chick that Fu had knocked into. Shorty looked visibly scared of him and he played off that shit. I checked him once we got into my sister's juice bar about the shit too. I even noticed that when we were leaving, she was sitting on the side of the building. Something about her stuck with me but I couldn't put my finger on it. What the hell was she doing there anyway? Her clothes looked a little ragged, but that didn't mean anything.

When I saw her sitting with this sad look on her face, my wheels started to turn as usual, so I decided to call Kayla.

"What do you want, bighead? I'm trying to close up shop," she answered.

"Kay, I need you to do something for me really quick."

"What Game? You know a sister is tired. Don't be putting me up to no shenanigans."

"Man, do I ever put you up to shenanigans? Now listen really quick. I need you to go outside and look on the side to see if a girl is there. She's kind of brownskin wearing some dingy ass clothes."

"What? Are you serious?"

"Yes, I'm dead serious. Now go!"

"Okay, okay," she said, and I could hear her moving.

"Yeah Bro, it's a girl out here sleeping on cardboard. I wonder where she came from? I've never seen her."

"Man, me either, but she don't need to be out there like that. It's damn near thirty degrees out."

"I know, but we can't do anything about that. We don't even know her."

"It doesn't matter that we don't know her Kayla, she needs help," I said sternly.

"There you go Jahfar! Always trying to save somebody. You need to mind your business sometimes!"

"Kay, I'm not trying to hear that. Now listen, this is what I need you to do…"

Kayla Gambino

I got my day started at 5 am with my morning run, yoga and breakfast. My brother, Game, always taught me that the earlier you woke, the more you had to gain. I'd lived by that mantra since I was fifteen and it hadn't steered me wrong yet. I slid on some American Eagle jeans, a fitted V-neck shirt and my chestnut Uggs so that I could get ready to go to the K-Spot. The K-Spot was my baby. I ate, bathed and slept the K-Spot. I always got there before anyone else, and was the last person to lock up. The K-Spot was not only a vegan juice bar, but it was also was a chill spot for geeks like me.

There were several special reading rooms with soothing lights and relaxation crystals. So not only could you get yourself a cool, refreshing drink, you could also zone the fuck out. My baby had been thriving for the last six months and I owed it all to my brilliant big brother, Game. Game was the only one of us who'd graduated from college. Jalen spent most of his time in and out of prison, Danni got involved with some fool and had millions of kids, and my youngest brother, who was something like a miracle baby being that my mother had him at damn near fifty, was still in high school. Me, I didn't know what I wanted to do, but Game let me know that I had to do something even if I didn't want to go to college.

Game even fronted me $50,000 and the rest was covered in a bank loan. Now, here I was. I unlocked the doors to the K-Spot and it was just as spotless as I had left it. But I remembered that I had something to do for Game. I got some breakfast started, which consisted of fruit, muffins and freshly squeezed fruit juice. Once I was done, I went outside to wake up the sleeping woman. I called out to her, but she didn't respond. I then gently shook her and she jumped up.

"Sorry," she said quickly. "If you want me to leave, I will go. I don't want any trouble."

"No, no," I said." You don't have to leave. I was just wondering if you wanted some breakfast." She looked like she was thinking before she shook her head no.

"Okay. Well I'm Kayla and this is my place. I have some extra breakfast left over and I just didn't want it to go to waste," I lied. "How old are you?" I wondered who would leave their kid to fend for themselves like this. It was cold as hell outside and she was sleeping on a cardboard box.

"I'm twenty-five."

I gasped when I heard her age. This girl was so tiny that I thought she was about sixteen or so. Now I was in 'save-a-hoe' mode just like my brother.

"Oh, okay." I tried playing it off. "Well, if you don't want to eat at least come in so that you can get warm. I promise I won't hurt you," I assured her.

She looked for a few moments before she finally got up and followed me inside. For a homeless person, she didn't have a bad scent and though her clothing was filled with holes, they were clean.

"You can sit here," I said, directing her to a table. We wouldn't be opening for a few hours, so she was good. I brought out the food for her and now I felt like I needed to make more. I was around her age and couldn't imagine my life being anything like hers.

She stared at the food at first before slowly giving in. She started off slow, but then eventually stuffed her mouth as if the food would disappear. She saw me looking at her and then slowed down.

"Anna," she said, while taking a sip of juice. "My name is Anna."

"I don't mean to be in your business or nothing, but why are you sleeping outside? Where is your family?"

"I don't have any family. It's just me. My mom died when I was little, and my father is off somewhere."

"Sorry to hear that," I expressed.

"It's okay. It happened a long time ago. Do you mind if I use your restroom?"

"Sure. It's right through there." I pointed to the back. She left and I grabbed my phone to text Game and tell him about Anna. Anna emerged from the restroom about five minutes later. When she walked past, I smelled the scent of mouthwash.

"Well, thank you for everything."

"Kayla."

"Kayla, thank you for the breakfast and for letting me use your restroom. I don't want to take up too much of your time, so I'm going to go. Thank you again."

With that, she didn't even let me respond before she dashed out of the door. Ten minutes later, I went to check on her and she was gone. I had a feeling that she was used to running, so she wouldn't be coming back.

Game Gambino

I was parked at my and Bregan's meet up spot when I got a text from my sister, Kay, about ole girl that I told her to check on. Shit was crazy how so many people could have so much, while others had so little. Baby girl even left before we could do anything, so for now we had to just let that situation be.

Bregan pulled up in a white-on-white Tesla, and as soon as she parked, my girls, Ava and Logan, popped out and ran to my car with their mom walking behind them.

"My babies," I said while pulling them in for a hug.

"Daddy, I have my Christmas list already for you," my youngest, Logan, said.

"I'm sure you do." I laughed. "And what's on it?"

"Training bras," my oldest blurted out and started laughing.

"That is not fair. Daddy, tell her to stop please," Logan whined.

"Aite y'all, go and get in the car and figure out where we are eating tonight."

The two both ran to the car, leaving their mom and me alone.

"How have you been Jahfar?" she asked.

"I'm straight," I replied, and then there was silence.

"Oh, so I guess you don't care how I've been," she stated with an attitude.

"Come on man, you can answer that for yourself."

"Okay, so Jahfar you know that we have to co-parent until these girls are eighteen. It's been two years. When are you going to forgive me so that we can move on?"

"Man, I'm not trying to hear all of that. My kids are old enough that they can talk to me. You and I don't even have to communicate at all."

"See, it was you and this stubbornness right here that drove me to do what I did. It's your way or the highway and that shit is not gone get you far."

"Well how far is far enough away from you? Huh? It's funny that you want to be Chatty Cathy now, but when you were out sucking niggas' dicks you ain't have nothing to say."

"Jahfar, please don't try to play me. Yeah, I stepped out on you and I was wrong for that, but I had to get it from somewhere. You didn't want me and paid me no attention. It felt like I was just a distraction at first until you didn't need me anymore for you. Is that what I was?" she asked, damn near touching my face with her finger.

"Yo, chill the fuck out before I embarrass you in front of our kids. What would you have been a distraction from?"

"FROM YOU! I met you when I was fourteen, but whatever happened before I came into the picture really fucked you up. I think me and all my problems helped you escape from yours for a while, and then after you put all of your demons aside and fixed yourself, you didn't need me anymore. How many times did we even have sex the year that I had Logs? Five, six times? Don't try to play the victim here Jahfar. I was wrong to step out, but you are not faultless in this situation. Oh, and let's not forget, you stepped out way before I did," she laid into my ass.

"You finished or you done? Because I don't have time to hear this shit," I said, walking off. No matter what she said to try to justify her actions, she was the one who fucked up. Yeah, I cheated a few times, but that was when we were petty ass kids and before my daughters. When we were grown enough to establish something real, Bregan was the only woman I needed. But the same couldn't be said for her. I still loved Bregan for the sake of my kids, but shit would never be the same between us. We could never go back.

"Boy, I know you're not just going to walk past me," Chi Chi from the South side yelled to Fu Fu.

"Girl, gone 'head and leave me alone," he yelled.

"Yo, didn't you fuck her a few days ago? Why are you fronting on her?" I asked my friend.

Rod was doing a stint in Juvie and Fu had moved to the hood after he left.

"Yeah man, but I don't want her to be my girlfriend or nothing like that. She's worrisome as hell," he said, wiping the sweat that formed along his brow. It was another hot ass summer, but we loved it.

"So, you don't hear me talking to you Fuquan!" she yelled out his government name which cracked me up because he hated that shit.

"Girl, fuck you!" he said, flicking her off. "Oh, too bad I already did that, hoe!"

"Who are you calling a hoe?" Her friend stepped up for her. "I know you're not calling my cousin a hoe!"

That wasn't even her damn cousin.

"Aye shorty, mind your business. This is between him and her," I butted in.

"Lil' boy, who is you?"

She pranced over to us wearing some hot pink shorts and a white halter top. Her hair was in this crinkly style with the colorful butterfly clips all throughout.

"Lil' GIRL, it's who ARE you? With your dumb self," I corrected her.

"Boy, you need to correct Dee and not me!" she said, with her hands on her hips.

"Who the fuck is Dee?" Fu asked, "'cause me and my guy will fuck his ass up."

He put his arms around my shoulders.

"DEES NUUUTTTS!" she and Chi Chi said together and busted out laughing walking away.

"Yo, who is that?" I asked, talking about the new girl who I had never seen that claimed to be Chi's cousin.

"Man, she ain't nobody. I think her name is Bregan or something! Her fine ass."

Fu was right. She was dope as hell and she wore the newest Jordan's with her outfit. It didn't hurt that she had this little pudgy face, sort of reminding me of the girl from Love and Basketball when she was little.

"Yo, you need to be nice to Chi Chi so she can put me in deep with her."

"Man, hell no! Chi is too crazy, and she's been acting dumb since I took her virginity. Bitch was bleeding all over my sheets."

"Nigga that ain't nothing. You do know that you popped the cherry if it was her first time."

THE REALEST IN THE GAME WANTS HER

"Yeah nigga, but that shit is nasty. You on your own with her and Chi Chi, bruh."

"Man don't worry about it. I can get her on my own," I said, walking off and leaving him. Bregan was gone be my girl whether she knew it or not. Just watch, she was gone be mine.

My girls arguing knocked me out of my thoughts as I looked in the rear-view mirror and they were shoving each other. Ava was thirteen and Logan was nine, and they could not get along for more than five minutes.

"Logs, stop patronizing your sister and Ava, chill out with the attitude," I said, scolding both of them.

"Ouuh, someone had a grumpy salad today," I heard Logan tease me.

"Yep, and they had extra grumpy dressing," Ava joined in.

Now they were getting along at the expense of me. I only chuckled and continued to drive to nowhere since the girls couldn't decide where they wanted to eat. This weekend would be full of laughing, crying and arguing so I needed to prepare.

"Have y'all decided where y'all want to eat? Or do y'all want oodles of noodles?"

"Ewww Daddy, Mom says those are for people who live in the ghetto."

"Well, maybe yo' mama forgot, but she used to live in the ghetto."

"Well Daddy, not to undermine the ghetto, but I would much rather have Chipotle," my sassy nine-year-old said.

"Chipotle it is, even though I thought that we would go to a sit-in restaurant."

"Daddy, it's late. We just want to eat and go home to watch Netflix," Ava commented. "Oh, and has Marisol cleaned my room yet?"

I shook my head at my spoiled daughter.

"No, she didn't clean it. That is your job. What do I pay you allowance for?"

I was about to go on and on about how hard work paid off when Logs stopped me.

"Oooh Daddy, look at that lady laying on the cold ground. Can we help her, pleeaaase? You always say that charity is the greatest of all. Annnnddd she's black."

"Baby, what does her being black have to do with it?"

"Welll, if she was white, I would say keep it moving because she has her own kind that can help her."

Damn, I was thinking I had been talking around her for too long because she was starting to adopt my way of thinking. I mean, I wasn't a racist, but I was all for MY people.

"Baby, when giving and helping someone, their skin color shouldn't matter, okay? It's okay to be for your people, but you still don't treat others badly."

I stared out of the window at the familiar face laying on a park bench. It was the same woman that was outside of Kay's store. I guess she had relocated so Kayla wouldn't bother her anymore, but that didn't work out so well.

I walked over to her with the girls on my trail after they begged to come with me. Laying on the bench, her face was buried in her hoodie, shielding her from the cold. I tapped her lightly and she jumped, causing the girls to jump as well.

"This is public property. I am allowed to lay here," she protested before I could even say a word.

"Shorty, I'm not trying to bother you, but it's cold out here. Let me get you a hotel room for the night."

"Umm, I'm good," she said, never making eye contact with me.

"Look, I know you don't like being helped, but I can't leave you out here tonight. It's not safe out here, baby girl."

She looked weary.

"Come on, we can help you. My daddy is a nice man. He won't hurt you," Logan said, gently grabbing her hand. She grabbed her things and then followed us to the car. The car ride was quiet, and she still didn't make any eye contact with me.

"You mind if I ask your name?" I asked.

"Your sister didn't tell you already?"

"Nah, she didn't."

"It's Anna."

"Oh, okay. Well I was just about to take my daughters to get Chipotle. Would you like some?"

"What's that?" she asked, finally looking up at me.

"Oh my god, only the best place ever. They sell like rice bowls and wraps and stuff," Ava chimed in.

"Ohh, sounds healthy," Anna replied.

"Tuh! Hardly!" I said, negating that healthy comment.

"Ohh, well I will take whatever. It's fine."

"Okay, girl. I will hook you up. Be right back."

The girls and I went in and Anna stayed in the car. We came back about ten minutes later. The aroma of the food filled the car and I heard shorty's stomach rumble. I wondered if she had eaten since the day Kay gave her food.

"You can eat in here if you want to," I told her.

"Ohh, it's okay. I don't want to spill anything."

"Oh, it's fine. Our dad gets his car cleaned at least twice a week. We spill stuff all the time," Logan said.

She laughed a little, but quickly stopped as if she didn't deserve to laugh. I peeped it all. About twenty minutes later, we arrived at the Marriott hotel and I checked her in. She offered me a simple thank you and then scurried along. The wheels were now starting to turn in my head again.

Kayla Gambino

I texted Game to make sure that I had her correct room number as I had been knocking for a few minutes and gotten no answer.

I know this girl didn't run away again.

Game let me know that it was indeed room 112, so I knocked harder before the door was finally opened. Anna had on a white terry cloth robe as she wiped the sleep out of her eyes.

"Is it time for me to check out?" she asked meekly.

"Well, not quite, but I would like for you to get your things and come with me." She looked at me skeptically.

"Look, you can't afford to stay cooped up in this hotel for too long so let me help you. You don't have to feel no type of way about it because I was in your exact place before," I lied, hoping that she would let me help her if she thought that we had something in common and I wasn't judging her.

She got what little she had and rode with me to the K-Spot.

"Why are we here? she asked. "Oh my god, are you going to give me a job?" she asked excitedly.

"Wellll, right now I have enough staff, maybe too much, but I do have something else for you." We walked to the back where I had a spare room. I opened the door and she looked like she was wowed. My small storage room had been transformed into a nice little chill spot. It had a flat screen TV on the wall, a shaggy black rug on the floor, an air bed and a mini fridge.

"Is this for me?" she asked lowly.

"Yep. It isn't much, but it is a stable place for you to lay your head until you get on your feet."

"Oh my god, thank you so much." She hugged me so tightly and cried a little. I could tell this girl had really been through a lot.

"Now I'm trusting you with my baby here, so please don't do me dirty."

"I promise, I won't. And anything you need me to do around here, I will do for free." She cried before sitting down in a bean bag chair. Her tears were pouring so I left to let her have her space.

I walked out just in time to spot Danni coming in. "What's up girlie," I greeted her, but stopped abruptly. "Girl, what the fuck happened to your eye? Did that nigga touch you?

"No girl. I was playing with the kids and got elbowed."

"Are you sure?" I asked, passing her an ice bag.

"Yes I'm sure, so don't go running to Game's crazy ass," she said defensively.

"Okay. You still at Mama's house?"

"Yep, 'bout to carry my butt back home. I'm tired of being mad at Mario."

"Girl, you need to be mad at him forever. Burn that house down, why don't you."

"Girl, you've never been in love before so I wouldn't expect you to understand."

"Well, you can throw all of your little greasy insults at me, but keep that same energy with Adonis Johnson," I joked, referencing the character played by Michael B Jordan in the movie *Creed*. Danni and Mario were always fighting about something.

"And by the way, I have me a little side thing, but I'm trying to be on Lauren London's level of privacy, so he will be kept under wraps until the time is right."

"Girl, you always been so sneaky. But anyway, are you coming to Sunday dinner? You know Mama is in an uproar about you missing the last two."

"Yeah, I will be there since it's my time to pick what she cooks. And you guys better be ready because it will be vegan."

"Oh gosh, now I know I'm really going back home to my man!" Danni laughed. She left and I got back to tending to my business.

Misty Blue

I'd been at the K-Spot for a few days now and things were going smoothly. Kayla had even brought me some clothing that she couldn't fit anymore so that I could go on job interviews. I didn't want to be seen as a charity case, but I wouldn't turn down the help when I really needed it. During the day I wouldn't just sit around on my ass, but instead, I got a library card and filled out at least twenty applications daily. So far, no one had emailed me about an interview, but I felt that my luck would soon be changing.

I sat in my new room reading *Sacred Woman,* by Queen Afu, when I heard a light tap on the door.

"Come in," I answered.

In came walking the stallion of a man whose name I still didn't know yet.

"Hey, just checking in to make sure that everything is good with you. I hope my sister didn't scare you by kidnapping you and bringing you here," he said with a smile. A perfect smile.

"Oh yes, I'm good. And thank you for your graciousness. I really appreciate you and your sister. I'm looking for jobs now, so I won't wear out my welcome."

"No thanks necessary, but what are you reading?"

I showed him the book.

"What is it about?" he questioned, leaning his toned body up against the wall.

"It's really a guide to healing your mind, body, and spirit from an Afrocentric standpoint. It promotes growth and positivity within oneself through positive affirmations and healing. I've actually read it three times already. It's one of my favorite books."

"Oh, it sounds dope. I might have to borrow it when you finish so I can try to understand y'all better."

"We are difficult creatures, aren't we? But what some of us possess is unmatched."

I felt myself getting a little too deep as he stared at me, so I shut up.

"You do that a lot, huh?" he asked after the brief silence.

"Do what?" I asked.

"Silence yourself. Since I've known you, you start but always stop. Why?"

"Because I don't have anything to say."

"You seem like you have a lot to say that you just choose not to."

"And that's my choice, right?" I snapped.

"Yeah, you're right, it is. I didn't mean to bother you. Guess I will see you around."

"WAIT! I'm sorry, I didn't mean to come off rude. I am really grateful for your help."

"So, what's your story? How did you end up where you are now?"

TESHERA C.

"I don't have a story and I guess I'm here right now in this moment because this is where I'm supposed to be."

She looked at me and there was something familiar in her eyes. It's like we'd met in a past life or something before.

"Well, good or bad, everyone has a story, and whenever you are ready to share it, there will always be someone to listen."

With that, he walked out.

I wasn't used to people being so nice to me and thought Kayla and her brother seemed like good people, but I couldn't be too trusting because there were some bad people in this world.

I ran as far and as fast as I could, finally stopping at the end of the street to catch my breath. My chest heaved up and down as I'd run for at least twenty minutes without stopping. I had been bounced around from foster home to foster home, and each time they got worse. I was fifteen years old and on group home number five. At least this foster mom did feed us, but when she was upset, her punishments were torture.

I felt the open scabs on my back, and they burned at the touch. I didn't have anywhere to go but before I knew it, I was back in my old neighborhood at Chandler's house. I rang the bell repeatedly praying that someone would answer. The door finally swung open and there stood Chandler, all grown up. I hadn't seen her since I was twelve years old.

"Misty! Is that you?" she said before grabbing me and hugging me tightly. I winced at the pain that she was causing to my back.

"Misty, what's wrong?" she asked, turning me around. "Oh my god, Misty! What happened to your back? Who did this to you?" She cried out so horrendously that her parents came to the door. "Mom, someone hurt Misty."

Ms. Arlene let me in and took care of me. She assured me that I could

THE REALEST IN THE GAME WANTS HER

stay with them and after the weekend, she would petition to become my foster parent.

It felt good as hell finally being back with the people who knew me the best. My dad and I stayed in our old house for a year after my mom died of a heart attack, and then one day he just never came home from work, leaving me alone. I didn't have any family besides my dad's family who were all still in Haiti. Soon after, I became a ward of the state.

"Dang Misty, I missed you so much girl. I'm so glad you're here," Chandler said. That night we laid in bed and talked all night. I shared everything that I had been through with her and we cried together promising to never leave one another again.

I had been staying with Chandler and her family for about two weeks when her big brother, Chase, came home from college. Chase was fine as ever with his light skin and dreamy eyes. He would always call me cutie and he told me that we would get married once I turned eighteen. I had a little crush on him, and Chandler knew it, so she teased me about it all the time.

One afternoon, I came home from school to find that I was all alone. Chandler had stayed after school for cheerleader practice and I guess her parents were just out. I put my things away and then went to the kitchen to make a sandwich. I got out everything I needed and then started to make it when Chase snuck behind me. I didn't even hear him come in the house because I had my earphones in.

"Oh my god, Chase! You scared the crap out of me." My heart was beating fast as hell.

"My bad girl. You don't have to be scared." He laughed. "Where everybody at?"

"I don't know. When I came in no one was here," I said, piling lettuce on my sandwich.

"You know you filling out real nice in them clothes that Mom got you," he said with a smile. He walked up to me and then palmed my face gently.

"When you gone become my girl?"

I laughed. "Chase, I'm fifteen and you are twenty. I know you have older girls chasing you around at college," I said nervously.

Chase and I had flirted before, but we never took each other seriously.

"Look, stop playing with me Misty," he said, grabbing my breasts and squeezing them.

"Wait, Chase. What if your parents come home?" I asked anything so that he would stop.

"Don't worry, they won't," he said, tugging at my jeans. He then ripped open a condom and put it on before pumping in and out of me. I laid there crying but my tears didn't seem to faze him as he went harder and harder making grunting noises.

"Please don't," I said, barely above a whisper. It seemed like him pounding on top of me lasted forever. Once he was done, I ran out of the house, never returning again.

Kayla Gambino

"MAMMMMMAAA! Your favorite has arrived," I yelled, announcing my presence. Mama had the house smelling good as usual and I couldn't wait to tear it down. As usual, Danni was there sitting on the couch with her face glued to her phone.

"Yo, you didn't just hear me walk in? Acknowledge my presence when you see me. And where are my nieces and nephews?"

"Girl, yeah, I heard your loud ass. And I don't know, outside minding their business."

"Danni, just because Game bought Mama this big house doesn't take away from the fact that it's still in the hood. You need to be watching them while they are outside," I chastised her like I was the oldest. It was true though; the hood had gotten way worse since we were kids. I didn't know why Mama wanted to stay, so instead of Game buying her a house in the suburbs like we wanted, she found this grand ass house, but it was smack dead in the hood.

"Girl, my kids are fine. I need some me time too. Damn!"

Danni had three kids, an eight-year-old, a five-year-old and a two-year-old who was always with the oldest one.

"Girl, Tae is only two. He does not need to be out with Trey. Let that little boy have his fun sometimes," I commented.

"Kayla, the day you spit one out, then I will take your advice. Until then, kiss my ass."

"Girl, I wish," I started before my mother butted in.

"Y'all two do this mess every Sunday and this week I'm not for it. Kayla, go in there and snap them beans, and Danni, go and check on my grandchildren. They haven't been in here in an hour."

Danni reluctantly got up and went outside to find her kids. They probably were almost to Africa by now and it was forty degrees out.

Once Mama came to the kitchen, I was doing as she told me, snapping beans.

"And where have you been? You skipped the last two family dinners," she started in on me.

"Mama, I have a life and sometimes I just can't make it." I shrugged nonchalantly.

"Well, what could be more important than family?"

"My career, Mom. You know the K-Spot hasn't been open for too long, so I have to make sure that everything runs smoothly."

"Well, that's all fine and dandy. But you better start squeezing your mama in sometimes. You know I won't be here for too much longer."

This was Mama's way of guilt tripping me. She literally came with the 'I won't be here for too long' mess every time I did something that she didn't like.

"Alright Mama, I will try to do better. But anyway," I said, breezing out of that conversation. "I have a friend coming over for dinner tonight. Is that cool?"

"Yeah child. You know there is plenty of food for everyone. Don't tell me you finally bringing your guy friend here. You've never brought anyone home. You know we thought you were gay at first and scared to bring your little girlfriend home."

"Mama!" I shouted. "I am not gay."

Here we go. That was another reason why I skipped Sunday dinner. Everyone was always in my business about my dating life.

"Yo, Yo." My little brother, Cameron, busted through the back door, saving me from this conversation.

"Brody," I yelled, dapping him up.

"What's good Sis? You got me on them Yeezy's that come out next week?"

"Boy cur' your big self. I don't even have a pair of Yeezy's!"

My little big brother was sixteen, standing at 6'6, but was lanky with it. He had all the little girls going crazy because he was the star basketball player, and everyone just knew he was gone get drafted out of college.

"Oh Sis, we have to change that," he joked, taking orange juice out the fridge and drinking from the gallon. Mama didn't even say anything. When I was younger, she would've back slapped me for that.

About an hour later, after chopping it up with Mama and cooking, everyone else started to pile in. Our Sunday dinners didn't just consist of us; the rest of my ghetto ass family came. Mama's sisters and all their kids and grandkids, boyfriends and some more. At the end of the night, it would be about twenty of us. Most of the kids were outside being terrorists, while the adults played cards and talked shit.

I walked out of the bathroom to see my guest arriving.

"Hey Anna. How are you doing? Did you find it okay?"

"Yeah. Thanks for inviting me," she said lowly.

This girl was so mousy and I was sure that my family would make her even more nervous. I had to admit though, she looked better than when I first met her. She had gained weight since she was eating now, and the things that I gave her fit her perfectly. Some of the stuff was brand new and had been hanging in my closet. Today she wore brown leggings and an orange, oversized sweater with a huge black belt around it. She topped it off with chocolate-colored, Vince Camuto knee boots. Her hair was up in a bun showcasing her round face. I had never looked at her really well, but she was beautiful, favoring that girl Ryan Destiny from the show *Star*.

"Y'all, this is my girl Anna. Anna, this is everybody."

"Hi," she said shyly before I took her to the kitchen to speak to my mom.

The two of them spoke and Mama told her how pretty she was. Anna then excused herself and went outside. I guess she needed some time to herself.

Misty Blue

I walked outside just to clear my head a bit. A sadness washed over me seeing Kayla's family. They all seemed so close knit and it just got to me how my family was taken away from me at such an early age. Flashbacks of seeing my mother laying on the ground with blood running from her head haunted me. Back then, I didn't even know that she'd died from a heart attack. I couldn't remember much from that night or a little before it. The doctors said that it was trauma-related amnesia. I would have flashbacks of seeing my mom and being assaulted, but I couldn't recall any details or who did it. I could barely recall anything that happened days prior.

Why did some people have these big loving families and I didn't? Why were my parents taken and all these other people had theirs? I felt myself getting hot as my nails pierced the inside of my hand. I could feel the blood spreading. Over the years, I had developed quite the mean streak, but it was a part of me that I didn't like, so I tried my best to hide it.

"Game, Game!" I heard being yelled and when I looked up, kids were flying towards the shiny car that had just pulled up. I was surprised whoever it was could get out of the car the way people flocked to him, even grown men. I squinted my eyes just a little and recognized Kayla's brother when three women whizzed by me.

"There goes that fine ass Game. What I wouldn't give to occupy his bed every night. My damn baby daddy would be in the dust if he ever chose me," the one with the leopard pants said.

"Girl, you know Game is picky as hell. He has bitches throwing pussy at him daily and he never bites. That bitch Bregan really broke his heart," another one chimed in.

"Well chile, I'ma just keep dreaming about his fine ass picking me up and letting me bounce on it."

They all started laughing and I caught Game, I now knew his name, as he was walking towards me, well, his mom's house. Kids were still following him, and it seemed like every woman was fantasizing about him.

He looked like someone out of a fantasy movie. His hazelnut-colored skin glistened in the sun and his beard was nice and fluffy, but neatly shaped. I didn't see a tattoo on any part of his body, which was cool because now-a-days, men were just marking anything on their body just to look down. His designer outfit hung from his 6'3 frame, but not too much like the little corner boys whose pants dropped blow their knees.

I stepped aside so that I would not block his way into the house.

"Aite y'all," he said to the group of young boys who were following him.

"I will be checking for those grades next week. You get $20 for A's and 10 for B's. I don't want to see no C's, especially if you didn't tell me that you needed help in that subject."

"Okay Game, bet!" one said, and then their smiling faces all ran off. It made me smile a little inside.

"Anna, right? How are you doing?" he said once he finally got to me.

THE REALEST IN THE GAME WANTS HER

"I see Kayla done dragged you to one of our eventful family dinners." He smiled.

"Hey. Yeah, she did," I said, playing with my fingers.

"Yo! You're bleeding," he said, looking at my hand. "Come in here. I think Mama has a first-aid kit." We walked into the house and it was as if everything stopped. Everyone became quiet and gave him their full attention before dapping him up and acting as if they hadn't seen him in a while. It was like everyone gravitated to him and his mother beamed as she pulled him in for an embrace.

"Mama, I thought I was your favorite," Kayla said, pouting in the corner.

"PSHHH!" Game said, while mushing her and leading me to the bathroom. He pulled out the first-aid kit from under the sink and sat on the toilet, directing me to sit on the edge of the tub.

"Open your hand," he said, and I did so slowly. There were indentations from my nails, and I made a mental note to clip them.

"You did this to yourself shorty?"

I shook my head no, but something different came out of my mouth.

"It's a bad habit when I'm nervous."

"I know my peoples didn't make you nervous. They're a little crazy, but they're cool."

I didn't say anything because for some reason, my voice was stuck in my throat.

"I hope you're ready to eat," he said, breaking the silence, and when I looked down at my hand, he had patched it all up.

"Alright, you're good as new." He smiled. "But next time, hit a bag or something, anything but this." He put everything away and then walked out of the bathroom.

I walked out of the bathroom a few minutes later, and Mrs. West was putting the food out. I couldn't wait to eat. I was filling out applications at the library all day and hadn't eaten a thing. I spotted Game's rude ass friend walking in; the one who berated me for falling on his Timbs. He spoke to everyone, but I noticed that when he spoke to Kayla, his eyes lingered on her for a little longer and she smiled like a schoolgirl. I wondered if they were dating.

This was a big ass family with kids running everywhere and their mamas weren't paying them any attention. I met Danni, the other sister, but she was really short with me. And the baby brother kept smiling at me every time I looked in his direction. I may have looked his age, but I was definitely getting my weight up so that I could look like an adult for once.

We sat down to eat around 6 pm and before we started, Mrs. West made sure that we said grace. I bowed my head and closed my eyes.

* * *

THIRTEEN YEARS old

All the kids sat on the old-style porch while we waited to be called in for dinner. It was six of us and we were all around the same age wearing our pretty dresses and suits from church earlier that day. It was Easter Sunday and the church had an Easter egg hunt, in which I found four eggs, and one even had $5. So far, I had $18 and was saving up to get a House of Dereon outfit. I had priced pants and a shirt to be around sixty bucks. I figured it would take me a few more months to get it all.

"Aye kids! Dinner is ready. Y'all come on in here," Mr. Smith said kindly.

This was my second foster home and by far, the nicest. Mr. Smith was so kind and always gave us snacks, even when his wife said no.

The five of us lined up and came in the house single-file. Sam, my

THE REALEST IN THE GAME WANTS HER

foster brother, was just in a happy mood dancing all over the place. He loved Chris Brown.

"Sam, stop all that clowning around like you have ants in your pants," Mrs. Smith said, making all the kids laugh. Mrs. Smith looked at us with a 'don't play with me' look that silenced all of us. One by one, she handed us our plates and we took them to the table. Mrs. Smith was a little crazy, but her cooking was delicious. Tonight she had prepared chicken smothered in gravy, mashed potatoes and peas. In the oven an apple pie was baking, and I couldn't wait to eat it with some vanilla ice cream.

I was handed my plate and walked to the table slowly so I wouldn't drop it.

"Oooh, I need a napkin," Sam said, getting up from his seat and dancing back to the kitchen to get a napkin.

Sam pop locked by me like he actually knew what he was doing and accidentally knocked into me, causing me to drop my plate. The food went all over the place and gravy had gotten on my new pink dress.

"What is going on in here?" Mrs. Smith walked up and asked.

"Sam made me spill my food, but-but-but it was an accident," I said, looking into her cold black eyes.

"Well ain't no wasting food in this house so get down there and eat it!" she demanded. I looked at her to see if she was joking, but I knew she wasn't when she grabbed me by my neck and pushed me down to the floor.

"I said get to eating bitch. NOW!"

I quickly began to put peas in my mouth one by one and gagged on a dust ball. My choking didn't even move her as tears formed in my eyes.

"Oh, so you choking now? I can help you with that." She then stepped on the food, mushing it with her shoe. It all looked like mush now.

"Now, that will go down a little easier for you."

I looked at Mr. Smith and he shook his head like he wanted to say something but turned his head instead.

"And what are y'all looking at? Eat your damn food!" she barked at everyone else.

I sat there humiliated eating the food that Mrs. Smith had made for me with her shoe. That was just one of the many tortuous nights for the few months of my life with the Smiths.

"Baby, we have to get some meat on your bones," Mrs. West said, shaking me from my thoughts. She had piled my plate quite nicely with some of my favorite foods. She'd also made an alternate dish for Kayla since she was vegan. For the rest of the night, I watched enviously and a little admirably as the family interacted with one another, and the overall love that floated through the room. For a moment, I was content.

Danniece Gambino

I woke up with a hangover from hell after doing a little too much at Sunday dinner. That was the real reason my eye was black that day that I saw Kayla. My ass had fallen down drunk as hell and hit my eye. I was finally back home now with Mario and his ass was gone already. He worked for the city and was usually out by 6 am. I stretched wide before I checked my Instagram page and posted a picture with the caption,

Feels good to be able to sleep in while y'all hoes working for a minimum wage check. Kids good, bills paid, life is lovely. Y'all hoes can't relate.

"TREEEEEEEYYYYY!" I yelled. "Get your sister up and get her ready for school and then make Tae Tae a bottle."

"Yes ma'am," my oldest son answered.

"Oh, and pour me something to drink first and go to my car and get my cigarettes."

I turned on the TV to see if last week's episode of *Love and Hip Hop* was on. I just didn't get why Rashida stayed with Kirk's dog ass after he swabbed her damn son for his DNA. If Mario ever, I would kill his ass. Now Joseline, she was my type of bitch; never taking anyone's shit and quick to beat a bitch's ass.

Trey came in with my cigarettes and a big cup of Sprite.

"Thank you. Make sure you change my baby's pamper. I know you know he be wet. Y'all need to be ready in fifteen minutes so I can drop y'all off."

"Okay Mommy, can you make us pancakes this morning?" Trey asked.

"Uhhh uhh Trey, I don't feel good either. Y'all gone eat at school."

Trey walked away defeated, but I didn't have time to be making no pancakes when breakfast was free at school.

I walked down the stairs thirty minutes later and the kids were all bundled up in their coats. Trey was holding Tae Tae.

"Y'all look cute," I commented before I walked out to the car and they followed.

The school was only four blocks away, so we made it there in no time. I was about to pull off after the kids got out of the car, but I spotted that fine ass Fu walking his daughter into the school. I turned my hazards on and skipped his way.

"What's up, Fuquan?" I greeted him.

"Oh, what's up Danni?" he said, but didn't so much as look at me.

"Why are you in a rush? You can't talk to me or something?"

"Danni, I'm trying to get my daughter in so I can eat breakfast with her. You need something? You good?"

"Yeah, you know what I need, but I saw you checking out my little sister last night. Y'all got something going on or something?"

"Man, mind yo' business. That don't have shit to do with you," he snapped.

"It is my business if you're fucking with my little sister but didn't let me sample that dick first."

"Man, you are trifling. Where is your son? I know you didn't leave him in the car."

"Boy, chill the fuck out. I left the heat on. He will be fine."

"Danni, if you don't get your simple ass back to that damn car with your kid, I'ma whip yo' ass and then call Game so he can whip yo' ass again."

I didn't get why this nigga was trying to play me, but I didn't take his threats lightly, so I marched my ass to my car but poked my butt out a little just in case he was watching.

I dropped my baby off with my mama and until the kids got out of school, I would be chilling like a villain.

Fuquan Grimes

"Yo, I just saw your sister at the school. That girl is crazy," I said, palming her ass.

"Baby, I don't want to talk about my sister right now," Kayla said, kissing my lips as her hands slid lower and lower.

Baby girl was hot and ready like Little Caesar's pizza.

"What do you want, bae?" I asked her seductively.

"I want you!" she said bashfully.

"No, you don't. You want something else. Tell me what you REALLY want."

"I want my dick."

"Oh, it's your dick now? Well, take what belongs to you then."

I didn't have to repeat myself as she pushed me down on her bed. Her lil' ass thought she was tough.

"Ride yo' dick, bae."

Kayla was a buck twenty-five if that, and short as hell, 5 feet even, but she took pipe like a big girl. I had taken her virginity three months ago and ever since, she wanted it morning, noon and night. And I was there to handle that. Both of our sex drives were crazy, and the sex was always a smash. I had trained my baby well.

Guiding her hips, she slowly positioned herself on my pole, taking all nine inches. She let out a low moan and breathed out before winding her hips on my dick. The way we never broke eye contact and really vibed with each other was sexy as hell. Her slow winding increased as she was now standing on her feet hopping up and down on my joint. She even spun around with my dick still inside and started throwing her ass back like she played for the Brooklyn Dodgers. I smacked her ass right where my name was tattooed along with a little heart.

"Baby, I love this dick!" she said, panting.

"You love this dick, huh?" I smacked her ass again. She was already light, so I left red hand marks on her ass.

"Baby, I'm about to cum!" she screamed out and then remained totally still. This was what she always did when she was about to nut. My dick touching her walls was the best feeling and we loved to relish in it for a moment.

Before she could cum, I flipped her ass over on her back and spread eagled her legs. Her legs made the letter V and her juicy peach pulsated in front of me. I dove in her juices and they splashed on my face. Her juices tasted like water just the way I liked it. Kay could squirm all she wanted but she wasn't getting away that easily. I trailed back up to her mouth letting her taste her own juices before spreading her legs as wide as they could go and fucking the shit out of her. I went in and out of her ferociously and she was making these crazy ass faces that I loved; eyes rolling in the back of her head, biting her lip, and some more shit.

"Uhhh yes! Fuck me Fuquan! FUCK ME!" she yelled out. I came and collapsed on her body breathing heavy as hell.

"Damn Fu, that's that shit. If I ever catch you giving my dick away, I'm killing you, me, and her." she said, rolling over and taking a sip from her water bottle.

"Yeah, get your strength back and drink that water, Sista Soldier. You know you have to take your ass to work."

"Actually, that's my establishment. I don't have to do anything!" she said smartly.

"Okay boss, well show me how your mama made you a nasty hoe then."

She snapped her neck back giving me a look, and all I could do was hold my hands up and surrender. Kayla was young but didn't play that disrespectful shit.

She then got this look in her eyes and I knew that she was about to bless me with her mouth. Boy it was good to be me, FU-MUTHA-FUCKIN-QUAN!

Game Gambino

"What's up Fu?" I answered my ringing phone. I was on my way to a staff meeting at the office and everybody was blowing me up. Christmas was a week away and it seemed like everyone had their Christmas list ready for me like I didn't have two daughters to look out for.

"What up Cuh? Hell you doing?"

"On my way to Microsoft. What's up with you?"

"Man, you know me. Out here getting this money." Fu had his own construction company. He and I both used to be in the streets selling drugs, but that shit got old quick and we had to switch it up. Don't get it twisted, we were still thugs at heart, but we also knew how to trade in our Balmain jeans for business suits.

"Man, when you gone be truthful with me? I know you and Kay got something going on. Why y'all sneaking around?"

"Man we're not sneaking, but she is special to me so I want to keep her close. We're not hiding, but I'm glad you're not mad about it, Bro."

"Nah, I'd rather you with my sister than any of these other cornballs 'round here."

"Yeah, I feel you on that one Cuh. But before you hang up, the girl that Kay brought to Sunday dinner, give her my apologies for being a fuck nigga when I first saw her. Kay laid my ass out for that shit."

"Aite man, I got you, but I'm about to head in this meeting, so I'll catch up with you later."

"Aite Bro. One," he said, ending the call.

I PRESENTED my new autism awareness game to the Microsoft experts and they ate that shit up. They loved it and with a few minor tweaks, the game would be dropping in the summer. It felt lovely to be recognized for the shit that I did. It also didn't hurt that I would getting a $100,000 advance along with 50% of all sales. Life wasn't too shabby for me.

I cruised to Nipsey Hussle's *Victory Lap*, bobbing my head to his flow. This nigga was underrated as hell, but low-key was one of the best rappers out of LA. I got caught behind a city bus and noticed Anna standing waiting for another bus, I guess. She had her head down in her book not even paying attention to her surroundings. One thing I couldn't miss was the way her ass was sitting in the skirt that she was wearing. Baby had to be at least a buck forty now, which was different from when I first met her, because she was no more than 100 lbs soaking wet.

I beeped my horn at her, and she looked in my direction and waved. I waved her over and asked if she needed a ride. Surprisingly, she said yes and hopped in. She was dressed in a grey pencil skirt, a white, ruffled button-up, and black pumps. Her hair was up in her normal bun and little studs sat on her earlobes.

"Where are you headed?" I asked, turning the blasting music down.

THE REALEST IN THE GAME WANTS HER

"Back to the K-Spot. I just left a job interview." She smiled a little.

"Oh yeah? It must've gone good for you to be smiling." I picked up on how she even glowed differently when she was happier.

"Well, I didn't just do good at the interview, I did great, and they offered me the job on the spot. You are now looking at your newest Starbucks barista." She beamed.

"That's what's up. Congrats," I said, sharing her joy.

"Yeah, it feels good to have someone believe in me enough to hire me."

"Yeah, I know how that shit feels."

At one point, I didn't have anybody who believed in me besides my mama and an old teacher, so I knew exactly the feeling that she was describing.

"Where are you coming from? If you don't mind me asking. You're all dressed up looking jazzy."

I was surprised that she was being so friendly today. Other times, I couldn't get her to say two words.

"Oh me? I just came from my job."

"Where do you work? If you don't mind me asking."

"I work as a gaming creator for Microsoft."

"Oooh, that sounds like a big deal. I guess that's where you got your name from, huh?"

"Well kind of. That's what most people think, but it's actually the only thing my dad ever bought me before he dipped on my mom. I carried my Gameboy around with me everywhere. I still have it to this day," I said, going back in time.

"Yeah, I can relate," she said, staring out the window a little sadly.

"So, what are you doing to celebrate your new job?" I asked, changing the subject that obviously upset her.

She shrugged. "I don't know. It's not like I just graduated from college or something. It's not a big deal." She minimized her small victory.

"Well, you should let me take you out to celebrate one day," I said, pulling up to her destination.

"Yeah. Maybe," she said shyly. Once again, she was back in her bubble just that quickly.

"Thank you for the ride," she said, and then leaped out of the car and into the store. She was going to be one tough cookie to crack.

Misty Blue

I had to get the hell away from Game because he was making me feel tingly things. Tingly things that I shouldn't have been feeling. Tingly things in places that shouldn't tingle. I would be starting at Starbucks in two weeks and luckily, Kay had already given me two pair of black pants, so that was all I needed until I got paid to purchase some more.

"Girl, why are you running? I saw my brother just drop you off," Kayla commented as she wiped a few tables. Even though Kayla hired help, she still did some of the work that she paid people to do simply because it was her shit.

"Yeah, he saw me standing at the bus stop and offered me a ride home."

"Umm hmm, you two just keep running into each other. You know my brother is feeling you right?" She stopped and gave me her full attention.

"He is not! What would he want with the poor, homeless girl when he's like, rich?"

"Girl, he is not rich. Wealthy and comfortable, yes. Rich, no." She laughed.

"Well, even if he's not, he's way too good to be checking for someone like me."

"Girl, someone like you? My brother has a type and it is hoes. You would be better than any of the people he's brought home; even his baby mama."

"Really? He doesn't look like the type to slum."

"Yeah girl, my brother has two daughters. I mean, his BM is cool, but got a lot of shit with her."

"Oh, okay," I said, not knowing why she was divulging all of this information.

"Girl, believe me when I tell you that my brother is definitely feeling you and he usually gets what he wants, so go ahead and prepare yourself."

I walked to my room thinking about what Kayla had just said. She was wrong as wrong could be because a man of Game's caliber would only feel like he had to help me because it was the right thing to do, not because he wanted to get to know me. I wasn't checking for him and he definitely wasn't checking for me.

Game Gambino

Christmas

Christmas wasn't like it was for me back in the day. When I was younger, I couldn't wait to get up to open the little bit of presents that I had. I would be up by 8 am knocking on the door for my mama to bring her ass. Here it was, 10 am on Christmas day, and my girls still weren't up. I was more excited than they were. I walked to Logan's room first because my baby girl was the one who had toys and shit to open. Ava only wanted clothes, shoes, a MacBook and them ear air pod shits.

"Loggy Logs," I said, snuggling up with her in the bed.

"What Dad?" she said groggily.

"Wake up. It's Christmas stinky butt."

"Dad, it will be Christmas all day. Let me sleep."

I laughed at this smart little girl and started to tickle her. That would get her butt up.

"Okay, okay Daddy! I'm up, I'm up." She laughed like crazy.

"Aite. Go brush your teeth with that dragon, funky breath."

"Oh, you're one to talk," she said, going in her bathroom and shutting the door. I had one up and one to go. Ava wasn't that hard to wake up once she heard she had the latest Balenciaga's under the tree.

I watched my babies tear through the expensive black and silver wrapping that the girls had to have all their gifts wrapped in, and I couldn't put a price on their smiles. All I heard was, *thank you Daddy, this is exactly what I wanted Daddy.*

I even copped baby girl a training bra that she begged me for. The girls went on playing around with their new gifts and I showered and slipped out for a minute. Chef Carry was there preparing breakfast and dinner and my little brother had come over to get the gifts that I had gotten for him. His big sixteen-year-old ass still got excited about Christmas. He didn't know that he cost me damn near $10,000 alone because of the grown man designer clothes and shoes that he wore.

My first stop was to Danni's so I could drop my nieces and my nephew's shit off. Their house was filled with wrapping paper and the kids looked happy as hell thanking Mario for their things. Mario wasn't even the oldest two kids' dad, but he treated them no different from his kid. My sister just sat there on the phone not even interacting with the kids. That shit pissed me off, so I dipped before I broke the fucking phone and stuffed it down her throat. My second stop was to each of my older brother Jaylen's, baby mamas' houses, and it was five of them shits. I couldn't wait until his ass got out next month so that primarily taking care of his kids wouldn't be left solely on me.

Lastly, I made it to my mom's crib and dropped off her and her husband Cliff's gifts. Cliff was the best damn stepfather. He was the one who taught me how to be a man. My mom met him when I was sixteen and he couldn't have come at a better time because I was spiraling out of control. I chopped it up with Mom and wiped her tears because I had gotten her these diamond earrings that she had been saving up to get for months. They cost a pretty penny too, but there wasn't anything I wouldn't do for my mama.

My last stop was to the K-Spot. I arrived just as Kayla was parking.

"Merry Christmas Jahfar! What are you doing here?" she asked.

"Oh, I came here to see you really quick."

"Well, where is my gift?" she asked like the spoiled brat that she was.

I pulled out a stack and put it in her hand. Kayla was all about the green. Her eyes lit up like she was twelve again before she jumped on me and hugged me.

"Aite now, Kayla. Get the fuck off me," I joked.

"Boy, whatever. I don't want to mess up that new Gucci sweater you're rocking, but Anna is in there. I know you didn't come here to see me because you didn't even know that I would be here. I came over to invite her to my place for dinner, but I guess that isn't necessary anymore, huh?"

She thought that she was so funny with that damn clown ass smile on her face. I didn't even answer her ass and went in without her.

Anna's door was closed so I knocked.

"Come in," she sang sweetly.

"Merry Christmas," I said after opening the door. She was sitting on a bean bag reading *The Color Purple*.

"Merry Christmas to you too," she said, kind of caught off guard.

"So, check this out. I'm cooking tonight at my spot. It will be just me and my daughters and I would like for you to join us. And before you say no, the little one put me up to this. She said, 'Daddy ask the lady that we picked up that night to come to our house. You know, the one who looked like a melanin queen.'" I did my best impersonating Logan with her little raspy voice.

She laughed. "And how could I say no to someone who described yours truly as a melanin queen? Sure, I will come."

Damn, I thought for sure that I would have to drag her out kicking and screaming, but shit went by smooth as hell. Anna mentioned that she didn't really have family, so I didn't want her to be alone on Christmas.

"Okay, so I will give you some time to get ready and I will send a car for you around four. Is that cool?"

"Yep, I will be ready. See you guys then."

Misty Blue

I was finally ready, but I was second guessing this whole dinner as my nerves started to get the best of me. I looked at myself in the floor-length mirror and wondered if the black, knee-length, backless dress was too much. I didn't want to overdress, but I also didn't want to underdress. I heard a horn beep outside, so I had to get going. I slipped on some patent leather pumps and a trench coat and made my way out. It took us at least forty minutes to get to Game's house and when we finally arrived, I had to do a double take.

"Sir, are you sure we're at the right house?" I asked the driver who continued to stare at me, but never said a peep.

"Yes ma'am. This is Jahfar Gambino's residence. You can close your mouth; your eyes are not deceiving you. Go ahead and walk right in. The door is unlocked."

I got out and slowly walked to this house that resembled a fancy hotel on the outside. What the hell did he need with a big ass house like this? Growing up, I thought we lived in the big house, but Game's house would swallow mine. I opened the door slowly and old school Michael Jackson "Santa Clause is Coming to Town" was playing. The house smelled of an intoxicating aroma, which meant that someone was throwing down in the kitchen.

Game's house was just as magnificent on the inside as it was on the outside. The floors were marble silver and white and Basquiat was hung on the walls. A 12-foot tree was lavishly decorated with black and silver ornaments and though I expected to see wrapping all over, the ground was spotless. I was learning that Game was a meticulous man.

I walked in the direction where the music was coming from and saw Logan coming down the swivel staircase looking as sweet as ever in her mint green dress with big ruffles down the bottom. Her hair was done in a half-up, half-down style, and she wore a tiara like the princess she was.

"Hey," she squealed. "I can't believe my dad listened to me and invited you."

"Yes, and thank you for the invite. Where is everyone?"

"This way," she said, grabbing my hand and practically dragging me. I swear this house was like a damn maze and each time I thought it would end, we just kept going. We finally made it to the kitchen where Game was seated playing Uno cards with his oldest daughter.

"Daddy, look who's here," Logan sang. Game got up to hug me and then took my coat and purse.

"Dinner will be served shortly," he said.

"Oh, and I like your hair. It looks good down."

I had finally straightened my hair and it fell past my shoulders. I usually wore it up though.

I spoke to Ava, but she really didn't say anything to me, so I just sat down.

"Would you like some wine?" Game asked.

"Yes, that's fine."

"Red or white?"

"What's the difference?" I asked, dumbfounded.

"Well red is usually drier and made from cherries and fruit like that while whites can be a little sweeter."

"Okay, I will try red."

He poured me a glass and handed it to me. I took a big gulp hoping to taste cherries, but the shit was so bitter that it made me cough.

"Oh my god, that's gross," I said, sticking my tongue out.

"I told you it was dry." Game laughed. Let me pour you some white."

"I don't think I need anything else. That nasty mess was enough." I laughed.

I tasted the second glass that he poured me, and it was way better with a little sweetness to it. A chef then came out from Game's second kitchen and let us know that the food was ready. We all went to the dining room and it was a spread set for a king. There was turkey, ham, macaroni, greens, potato salad, cornbread stuffing and some more. Other than eating at Game's mom's house a few weeks ago, I hadn't had a spread like this in years.

"I thought you said that you were cooking?" I turned to Game.

"Whaaaat? My daddy doesn't cook, but he does order take-out well." Logan laughed, giving me the scoop.

"Thanks traitor. Thank you for telling my secret." He laughed.

Game then went around the table and pulled each of our chairs out. I was surprised when he came to me, but I just went with it while Ava kept giving me death stares. I got the feeling that she didn't like me. I was about to dig into the food when Logan grabbed my hand so we could pray. Game led the prayer and then we all dug in. There were a few jokes here and there, but it was pretty awkward seeing that Ava had a problem with me being there.

"Daddy, I'm done. May I be excused please?" she asked abruptly.

"You don't want dessert baby?" Game asked.

"No, I don't, especially while she's here," she mumbled, and I knew that it was time for me to go.

"I'm going to go. Thank you for having me over," I said, scooting out of my chair.

"Hold on, you don't have to go anywhere!" Game said to me.

"Yo, get your rude ass upstairs," he said, glaring at her.

She stomped her way up the stairs with him on her heels. Now, she would really hate me. I made myself useful and started to take everyone's dishes to the sink while Logan sat there stuffed like she was half asleep. She was too cute. After I put the dishes in the dishwasher, I covered the food and sat it in the kitchen, not sure if Game wanted any more. I was used to this kind of stuff because Mrs. Smith always made the kids do it after dinner. Actually, she made us clean the entire house while she sat and watched.

I looked at a sleeping Logan and lifted her big butt up to take to her room. I made it up the stairs without dropping her and peeked in various rooms until I spotted the one with Loggy Logs on the door. I put her down in her bed and helped her out of her dress before laying her down and covering her with her *Jessie* comforter.

I tip-toed out of her room and ran smack dead into Game.

"Oh, I'm sorry. I didn't ask you to walk around your home, but Logan was falling asleep, so I put her in her bed." I was whispering and I didn't know why.

"You got to stop doing that."

"Doing what?"

"Apologizing for shit." He was now invading my space and I felt his breath on my lip.

"Uhh, I think I'm going to need another glass of wine," I said, stepping back, and he smirked.

Game was so surprised when he saw that I'd cleaned up and put his food away.

"You didn't have to do that. That's what I have cleaning ladies for."

"Oh wow." I laughed. "You have your very own Florence."

"You're damn right," he said, passing me the glass of wine.

Game then led me to the living room and we sat down on his couch. The fireplace he had was amazing. The flaming fire reminded me of the internal battle inside of me. The fire was beautiful, yet dangerous. One part of me was saying fuck it, I wasn't worthy of life, but another part of me said fight for my life.

I glanced over and Game looked like he was in his own world as well. His fists were balled and his eyes were set on the fire. I took this time to really take him in for the gorgeous man that he was. The rays of red and orange made his skin a delectable dark brown. I studied his masculine features. His jaw clench was almost hidden by his bushy goatee. He was a fine specimen, but I noticed a familiar sadness in his eyes.

"What's your story?" I asked, waking him out of his spell.

"Huh?" he asked, snapping out of his thoughts.

"I said, what is your story? You asked me mine, now I want to know yours."

"You didn't even tell me yours though, but I will tell you whatever you want to know," he said looking into in my eyes.

"Umm, what was your childhood like?" I turned away from his glare.

"Well, I grew up in the hood, dirt poor. My mom cleaned the hospital at night, and she had to do it by herself since my dad left. Shit was bad to the point that I have corns on my feet to this day because my shoes were so damn tight. But I had this teacher who made me see shit differently. He always looked out and made sure that my grades were A1. But something happened to him and then I turned to the streets, following in my brother's footsteps selling drugs.

"I really did some shit in my past that I wish I could take back. I hurt some people who really had love for me and sometimes that shit takes a toll on me. I felt like I was drowning until I met my girls' mother in high school. We both had our own problems and helped each other through, but even she wasn't enough. There was just some shit I had to work out within myself."

I nodded my head at his truth, unaware of what to say.

"Alright, now you can quit being so secretive about yourself. I know you have shit you want to say, but you don't trust anyone. You can trust me."

I thought about what he said, and although I was extremely guarded, I needed to let someone in.

"Well, I had the perfect childhood up until my mom passed. I don't really remember a lot about my childhood just because my memory has erased all the bad things that happened. But I do remember that my daddy was my best friend and my mama was my biggest inspiration. I had two best friends, Chandler and Tia, and we were like three peas in a pod. I got joked so much because of my name. People always said it sounded like a stripper's name, but Chandler and Tia always took up for me."

"Damn, what's wrong with Anna? I mean, it kind of sounds like a white girl's name, but it's not that bad." Game laughed. "Now if your name was Candy Kiss or some shit, that would be funny."

"Well, Anna is actually a part of my middle name." I laughed because he was being stupid now. "My first name is Misty, Misty Blue. I started going by Anna during my teenage years just because Misty had been through so much."

Glass shattered on the ground as I realized that Game had dropped his glass.

"Dammit!" he said.

"Is everything okay?" I asked. It was like he had switched up or something.

"Yeah, my clumsy ass," he replied. "But it's getting late so I'ma go ahead and get a car to take you home."

"Ohhh, okay," I said, completely thrown. I didn't question it though. I had times myself when I flipped like a light switch.

My car arrived 15 minutes later and I left without even saying goodbye because I didn't want to bother Game. I was sure that I would see him again. Despite the rushed ending, this was the best Christmas I'd had in fourteen years.

Mario Cooper

I walked in the house the day after Christmas to see wrapping paper still scattered throughout the floor. I had just come from a long day at work expecting to at least have dinner on the table, but who was I kidding? Danni was never the type of girl to assume the wifely duties even though she didn't work in a pie shop. On top of that, I paid for the kids' entire Christmas and she had the nerve to be mad when I didn't buy her ass shit.

Today was the same as usual. I came home to her oldest taking care of my son, the house a total mess, and her laying on her ass gossiping on the phone. I greeted the kids and then went upstairs straight to her. That weak ass *Real Housewives* show was on and she was laughing her ass off. She was just like them bitches, but the poor version.

"Aye D, I need to talk to you for a minute," I said, taking off my boots. My dogs were barking, but I knew I couldn't expect anything from her ass.

"I mean now D, not after you're done watching this bullshit."

"Well what's I wrong with you? You had a bad day at work or something?"

THE REALEST IN THE GAME WANTS HER

"Nah, actually I didn't. Shit didn't start to sour until I came here."

"Here comes the bullshit," she said, rolling her eyes and getting out of bed. She had on a silk nightgown that fit her like a glove. I couldn't even lie, Danni was bad as hell. Her physical was what had kept me with her for the past two years. She was just the right amount of thick, putting me in the mind of Juju from *Love and Hip Hop*, the thickness and all. She put it down in the bedroom too, but I wouldn't let that shit throw me off my game.

"So, what do you have to say Mario?" She rolled her eyes to the sky like I was the one who sat home on my ass all day doing nothing.

"Shit has got to change D. I'm not happy and apparently you're not either. I'm holding the house down and lately you haven't been holding down what you're supposed to."

"'Mario, I'm not trying to hear that. The shit's not working because you don't want it to. Now you're trying to put the blame on me!" she shouted for no reason at all.

"See, this is what I didn't want to do. Chill the fuck out. You know the kids are downstairs and can hear everything you're saying."

"I don't give a fuck. They need to hear that you're trying to break up our family because you probably got a lil' side bitch somewhere."

I didn't even say anything. I just grabbed my suitcase out of the closet and began filling it with my clothing.

"You want to go, then go. Shit don't faze me and it's plenty willing to take your spot."

I still didn't say anything. I put as much in my suitcase as I could, and would get the rest later.

"I'm taking my son too, D."

"No the hell you're not!" She jumped in my face.

"And what the fuck are you gone do?" I challenged her. "I said I'm taking my son!"

A scowl on my face formed and she shut the fuck up and moved aside. I got Tae ready and was headed out the door.

"Mario, you're not gone take us with you? We want to go," Trey asked with tears in his eyes.

I felt so bad for him, but I knew D wouldn't let me take them since they weren't biologically mine.

"I will be back lil' man. It's going to be fine," I lied.

I dapped him up and then left. All I could do was shake my head at Danni and what she had become. On the way out, I heard Trey's cries grow louder and louder.

"Shut the hell up boy! That ain't yo' damn daddy!" I heard Danni yell before I finally made it to my car. Danny would never see my son again, and if I had to, I would definitely get CPS to get the other two out of there. She had better count her days.

Game Gambino

"Yeah bruh, the shit had me bugging. At first, I thought I was hearing things, but she repeated it. I can't believe that I didn't recognize her. It's been years, but still," I said, explaining how I found out who Misty really was. I'd never told anyone but Fu about the shit that Rod and I had done fourteen years ago. I tried to put it behind me, and I prayed that they were okay, but my prayers weren't answered.

After that shit happened, I didn't even talk to Rod's ass anymore, and it helped that he was in and out of Juvie. It seemed like every time I finally tried to get over it, it would haunt me again. Images of Mrs. Blue on the ground played out in my mind and tortured me. Misty's cries when Rod was assaulting her deafened my ears, and deep down inside, I never really forgave myself for not helping her. I called myself getting out of the game and going legit, all to prove that I was a good person, and now the shit was smacking me in the face.

My mind was all over the place wondering if I was the cause of Misty's unfortunate situation. She hadn't told me much, but was I the reason that she was homeless? Was her mom alive? Now I needed answers, or I would go fucking crazy.

"Bruh, did you hear me?" Fu said, looking in my face.

"Oh, what? What did you say?"

"I said keep that shit to yourself. Not forever, but now is not the right time to tell her. She's trying to get herself together and don't need shit else knocking her back down."

"Yeah bro, I feel you on that. I'ma give it some time. It's just so crazy that she doesn't remember me or who I am. She said she doesn't remember much from her childhood, but it just seems kind of odd, you know?"

"Yeah man. Who the hell forgets a name like Jahfar? Yo' mama was straight clowning when she named you that shit bro. But in the meantime, try to stay clear of her," he suggested with a chuckle.

"You out of your mind. Jahfar is way better than Fuquan. Yo' mama had to make your name match your daddy's. Floyd and Fuquan." Now I was cracking it up.

"Yeah, hold my nutz nigga. And make sure you don't go falling in love with that girl," he warned.

"I don't know about all that. It's something about her that makes me want to get to know her better, build a friendship, and maybe even something more."

"Nigga, that's guilt talking. You think being her savior will right your wrongs, but that girl is broken and needs to heal on her own. Ain't nothing wrong with being nice, but you can't get too hung up on this shit. She's damaged, and she might damage you."

I thought about the advice that he was giving me and some of it I agreed with, but the damaged part I didn't. Yeah, she had her flaws like we all did, but damaged usually meant beyond repair, and that wasn't a label I would have put on her or anyone. Rod, Fu, and I were the only people who knew what happened that night. Rod, of course, because he was there, but Fu simply because he was my right-hand man and I could trust him.

He and I sat outside of Kayla's spot when I saw who I now knew to be Misty rushing in from work. She wore a Starbucks smock and her ass was sitting right in the khaki pants that she wore. She held a bunch of papers in her hand too.

"Go in there and speak to her nigga. You know you want to," Fu joked.

He was right. My plan was to avoid her as much as possible, but she intrigued me and part of me thought helping her was what I needed to do.

I got to her just as she was plopping down in a chair. She looked worn out.

"Long day?" I said, startling her.

"You scared me," she said in a high-pitched laugh. "But yeah, today was long as hell. Someone called in sick, so my nine to three turned into a nine to six, but I won't complain. What are you doing here?"

"Well, I actually came to apologize about the way I acted the other night. I had just gotten a bad text and kind of overreacted."

"Is everything okay?" She sounded genuinely concerned.

"Yeah, it was about work. It had nothing to do with you," I lied.

"Ohhh ok, it's cool. I enjoyed dinner, but I get the feeling that Ava is not too fond of me."

"Well, Ava is Ava. She is definitely her mother's daughter. I apologize for her as well."

"Don't worry about it. But before you go, I have something for you. I wanted to give it to you on Christmas but couldn't."

She went into a bag that was in the closet and pulled out a little box.

"It isn't much, but it's a token of my gratitude."

I opened the little box and there sat some kind of stone.

"It's a Chrysocolla Crystal. It is a stone of prosperity, acuteness, and intuitive abilities. When I was little, I was really into crystals for healing and positive energy, but now I only have one from back then," she said, holding the necklace that was around her neck. Attached to it was a reflective type of stone.

"What does that one mean?" I asked.

"This is a moon stone, one of my favorites. It is a protective stone that offers healing and sacred feminine energy."

"Ooh, well thank you. This is a very deep gift. I've never had someone put so much thought into something for me," I said, embracing her for a hug.

The shit was crazy because just holding her, I felt a magnetic energy flow through me. Her touch was so delicate, yet so powerful that I didn't want to let go. I hadn't felt a thing for a female in years and was just with KoKo to pass the time, but I was feeling this one.

Misty Blue

I swear every time I thought that it would slow down at work, more people started to pile in. I had been working six days straight and to be honest, I was dead tired, but I wouldn't stop. I had been stacking being that Kayla didn't charge me any rent, and in a month or so, I would have enough for a down payment on an apartment. The only thing that would hold me back would be my credit history. I had lights and some more in my name because of one of my foster parents. I would have to find a private owner of something because although I was really grateful to Kayla for giving me a place to stay, I needed my own.

"Hi, how may I take your order?" I said with a smile to the next customer. My cheeks were hurting like hell from fake smiling all day.

"Hi, can I get a cinnamon dolce latte and a blueberry scone?" the woman asked, and something was so familiar about her sultry voice. I looked at her a little closer and could spot that beauty mark on her nose anywhere.

"Chandler," I called out lowly.

She just looked at me at first, and then I guess something clicked in her head.

"Misty? Misty Blue?" She sounded shocked.

"Yes. It's me," I said excitedly. I hadn't seen her since I left her home over ten years ago.

"It is you! How have you been?!" she yelled like she was equally as excited as me. We didn't even care that there were customers behind her. I quickly told the manager I would be taking my break and Chandler and I took a seat at a nearby table.

"Chandler, you look good girl. How have you been?"

She wore a tailored, wine-colored suit and red bottoms on her feet. Her short hair was cut in a bob and the purse that she was wearing I'm sure cost more than what I made in a month at Starbucks.

"Girl, I've been great. I'm into real estate now and I'm getting married." She showed me her ring.

"Congrats, and you are doing very well," I said a little sadly. I wasn't anywhere near Chandler's level of success. She noticed my mood shift.

"Misty, how are you? Seriously?" She touched my hand warmly. "One day you just up and left my house and I didn't know where you went. I was so sick worrying about you."

I debated in my head whether I should tell her about what her brother did to me. A part of me thought that she wouldn't believe me anyhow.

"I just left because I didn't want to continue to be a burden on you and your family."

My childhood best friend could see right through me.

"Misty, come on. You can be honest with me."

"Well," I said hesitantly. "It was your brother. One day when no one was home— "

THE REALEST IN THE GAME WANTS HER

Her head dropped.

"Girl, you don't even have to finish. My brother is in jail right now for molesting our cousin who has special needs." A tear fell from her eye. "Misty, I wish you would've said something instead of running. I would've been there for you. I'm sorry that happened to you." She gripped my hand tighter.

We were now crying together.

"How have you been since then?" she asked, and this time I was honest with her. I told her about the numerous foster homes I had been in, the homelessness and the current position that I was in. She just kept apologizing about her brother. I guess she felt if it wouldn't have happened, I could've stayed with her and been successful too.

"Well, I'm into real estate so I'm going to find you something even if I have to help you pay for it myself."

"Girl, you know you don't have to do that."

"Misty, you are my sister. I got you."

"Well, thank you. Enough about me"—I hated talking about me— "tell me about your husband to be."

"Well, he's not from our side of town. I met him at the skating rink when I was seventeen and the rest is history. Now he works as a defense lawyer and the wedding is set for next year."

I was happy to hear that so many good things were happening for her. At first it saddened me, but she deserved it and she was making a life for herself like a boss bitch. We wrapped up and exchanged numbers, promising to keep in touch. I left work feeling awesome that I had reconnected with my best friend.

I arrived home limping like a wounded animal. My dogs were barking after completing a double. All I wanted to do was soak in someone's tub and read a good book, but I only had access to a shower, so that would have to do. I pulled out my keys to unlock the store, when I felt a tap on my shoulder. I hurriedly pulled out my mace and turned to face whoever was trying me.

"Calm down Miss. No one wants to hurt you. I was actually asked to pick you up."

I noticed that it was the same driver who Game had sent for me on Christmas.

"Umm, and where are we going?" I asked sassily.

"I have no idea. I just have an address."

"Oh, well I'm good," I said, always one to think that everyone was out to hurt me.

"Just to let you know, I was instructed to carry you if I have to," he said with a smirk on his face.

"Well can I at least shower? I have been working all day."

"That is not necessary," he said, and then walked to the car. I couldn't believe that someone had scheduled my entire night when all I wanted was to get a good night's rest before my shift the next day. I reluctantly got in the car, and by the time we made it to our destination, I was knocked out sleep; drooling and everything.

"Ma'am, we are here," the driver said, gently shaking me.

I got up and was now standing in front of a closed library.

"What am I doing here?" I asked.

The driver only shrugged and instructed me to go in.

I walked in and bright light illuminated the room. The sight of the neatly stocked books on the shelves excited me. The walls were painted yellow and white, giving it a comfy feeling.

"You like it?" I heard the deep voice say, and when I looked up, there was Game on the second floor, looking as fine as ever. He stood there leaning on the wall in a Versace sweat suit, one chain, and his crystal.

Even from twenty feet below him, I could see his waves spinning like a rollercoaster.

"Yeah, I like it. But why did you bring me here?"

"You like books, right?"

"I love books," I corrected him.

"So, they are all yours. There are 7,403 books in this library, and they are all yours."

"How are they all mine?" I asked, surprised.

"Well let's just say they all fell in my lap. As a matter of fact, the entire library is yours to do whatever you please. You can keep it to yourself, or you can get it back up and running. It's up to you."

I stood there dumbfounded, not believing that this man had presented me with an entire library.

"I can't accept this," I said looking up, but he was gone. Now, he was walking down the stairs.

"You can't accept it? Or you won't?" he asked, now closing the gap in between us. He was looking me right in my eyes and there was no running.

"I can't!" I replied, trying to keep my hands from shaking. I learned at a young age that men only gave you things when they wanted something in return.

"Why not?" he asked.

"I don't deserve this."

"You gave me a gift, why can't I give you one?"

"Ohhh, so you're going to compare all of this to the little stone that I gave you?"

"It means something to me," he said, grabbing a hold of my chin. We were so close and the coconut smell on him filled my nose.

"Let me show you around," he said, breaking away from me. I wasn't sure if he felt what I was feeling so it was great that he got away from me.

We walked room-to-room, and each room was themed with the genre of the kind of books that were inside. The rooms included urban fiction, contemporary romance, sci-fi, fantasy, children's books, nonfiction, biographies and more. But when we got to the last room, my mind was blown to see a reading room with aqua lighting and reading goggles. Huge pillows sat on the floor and it just gave me such a cool vibe. If I could read in this room all day, I would. It was almost orgasmic.

I caught Game smiling at the way my eyes lit up like they did in the past once Sunday school was over.

"So, you gone take it?" he asked.

I still didn't want to, but I didn't know how to say no because he seemed genuine.

"I guess I am now a proud library owner," I said, jumping up and down. Shit was the best feeling.

"Okay, well we have to ride back to my spot to get all of the paperwork. And yes, it will be your name on it only. It's all yours," he assured me.

We hopped into Game's midnight blue Phantom and the heated leather seats felt so good against my body.

"The only thing I need now is a hot bubble bath," I accidentally said out loud, and he looked over at me with this look in his eyes that I could not read.

We made it to his house at 11:00 pm, and by this time, I was dead tired. I almost couldn't make it into his house. He went upstairs for a minute

THE REALEST IN THE GAME WANTS HER

and then returned with paper in one hand and towels in another. I looked at him and scrunched my forehead.

"I heard you say you wanted to soak in the tub, well I have four here. It's a private one down here, and you are more than welcome to use it."

"Oh no, I can't." I nervously laughed. I wondered why he was being so nice and giving to me.

"Look, I'm not a creep or a weirdo. Go ahead and relax."

He handed me the towels and pointed to the direction of the bathroom. The bathroom was cream and gold and the toilet looked like it was 24-karat gold. I looked at the fancy tub and it looked like a whirlpool. I ran the water and pulled lavender from my purse to put inside the flowing water.

After stripping naked, I stepped in the tub and the water was steaming hot just like I liked it. I hadn't relaxed like this in the tub since I was a little girl. In most of the homes I went to, we had timers in the bathroom because there were so many of us, or I had to hurry up and get cleaned before one of my step-dads joined me. But there was one home in particular that was not like the rest.

I sat in between Ms. Carolyn's legs as she braided my hair. I was the only kid that she had, and I wished that I could stay with her forever. I'd begged her for weeks to braid my hair in the new popular box braids, but she wouldn't let me until I turned sixteen. She even let me add a few pink strands to it.

"There child. You are done."

I hopped up so that I could check it out in the mirror, and the braids were like that.

"Thank you, Mama C. I love them." I hugged and kissed her cheek.

Tonight was the night of the spring dance and I needed to be there looking fly. Mrs. C had already bought me a Tommy Hilfiger halter top along with a blue jean jumper and high-top Air Forces. It wasn't even about the material things that she did for me, but Mrs. C really loved me. She told me I was beautiful daily, helped me to meet new friends, and took me to church every Sunday. But most of all, she made me believe that I was worthy and that she would always look after me.

"Okay, Mama. I'm about to go get ready for the party. My curfew is 11, right?" I tested her.

"If you come to my door after 10 pm, you may as well make yourself comfortable outside. Curfew is 10 pm, Miss Misty."

I laughed at the way she was always on point. Ms. C was just as beautiful on the outside as she was on the inside. She was in her early fifties, had a deep cocoa complexion and hair that she wore in a curly, medium-length 'fro. I hoped to age as gracefully as she did.

No soon as I got dress, my new friend, Stacy, was ringing the doorbell and telling me to come on. I kissed Mama C goodnight and made my way to the party. After having a blast and getting this boy's number, I raced back home with five minutes to spare before my curfew. I stopped at the end of the block to catch my breath and saw shiny red and blue lights flashing. I walked to my home slowly and it was blocked off.

"That's my house," I screamed from the tape that was blocking it off, and some man let me in. Before he could fix his lips to talk to me, I zoomed in the house only to see Mama C laid out on the floor.

"Oh my god, what happened to her?" I cried and was grabbed by a female officer.

"I'm sorry baby, but she is gone."

Those words hit my heart and my ears at the same time, and I broke down in the woman's arms. My crying spell lasted for weeks as I was bound to yet another foster home. I learned later that Mrs. C had a heart attack and that she had been dealing with some major health issues that she didn't tell anyone about. Both of my moms were now in heaven together.

THE REALEST IN THE GAME WANTS HER

The knock at the door caused me to jump.

"Aye, you okay in there? You didn't drown, did you?" I heard Game say.

I had been in the tub for at least 45 minutes and the water was still warm.

"No, I'm not okay," I answered, and he rushed in.

I smiled at the worried look on his face.

"Why are you playing?" he asked.

"I'm not playing. I'm not okay."

"So, what's wrong?"

"I want you to join me."

He stood there smirking in his sweats and his manhood let me know that he was thinking what I was thinking.

"You sure you want to go there with me shorty?" he asked seriously.

I thought for a moment before I answered his question. I liked him and it seemed like he liked me, so what was there to even think about?

"I wouldn't say it if I wasn't sure," I replied quickly before I changed my mind.

He dropped his pants and I wasn't even surprised to see the snake that was between his legs. He walked over to me and got in. I noticed that he had a tattoo on the right side of his chest with an elaborately drawn book, and on the front of it was the word Blue. I didn't even know he had a tattoo, but that wasn't what I was concerned with right now.

I crawled over to him and no words needed to be said. I was hungry and he was too. He picked me up and set me on his lap. He kissed me. This kiss I welcomed and the ones after that. He held me tightly because he knew I liked to run, but I wasn't going to run away this time. In one swift motion, he lifted me and sat me on his shoulders.

The minute his hands trailed up my back and scaled my bruises, he stopped. I knew he had questions, but he didn't ask them and kept at what he was doing. He was so focused that you would've thought he was going to win a prize or something as he buried his face in my mound. His entire face was in it, slurping and sucking my soul out of me.

"Oh my god, oh my god," I said lowly as he rolled his tongue slowly across my swollen clit. I had never orgasmed before and when I did, he caught all of it while biting the inside of my thigh. The next thing I knew he was slipping me slowly on his dick and it hurt like hell. I wasn't a virgin, but I hadn't willingly given myself away either. In my eyes, this would be the first, losing my virginity to someone I chose and wanted to do it with.

Game noticed the pain that was written on my face

"You sure you want to do this?" he asked, and I nodded my head yes.

He lifted me in his arms, and we got out of the tub and went to his room. He laid me down and started with his fingers going in and out of me. I was so wet that it sounded like someone was stirring some cheesy macaroni.

"Uhhh!" I screamed out because if this was the way his fingers felt, I could not wait to feel the real thing. He granted my request and piled inside of me, inch-by-inch. It really didn't hurt, but it felt more like there was pressure added. He stroked me slowly while he planted sloppy kisses to my lips. The pain was starting to subside and his strokes got longer and deeper.

Faster! I thought, and it was like he was reading my mind as he sped up, hitting every part of me, never breaking our gaze. By now, our sticky bodies were melting into one another and I felt myself cumming for a second time.

Harder! He read my thoughts again and hit it nice and strong. I was going out of my mind as I bit my bottom lip and kept up with his motion.

"Ahhhh shit girl," Game yelled out, and we came together. That night we were one. The feeling of him being inside of me was a feeling that I never wanted to go away.

THE NEXT MORNING, I was awakened by the pitter patter of feet running around. I looked at the clock and it was 12 pm. I had slept the night away but that was all Game. Suddenly my conscience started to kick in and I thought back to the past night. We went on exploring each other until the wee hours of the morning. I closed my eyes for a moment and images of him flooded my brain. How could something purely platonic end up being this? I was now second guessing it all. None of that was supposed to happen and I didn't want him to think that us having sex was some kind of exchange for the library that he had gifted me. My thoughts were running wild and now I felt ashamed and low.

"Oohhhhh, you stayed here last night in my daddy's bed," I heard Logan sing and when I opened my eyes, she was right in front of me smiling.

"Good morning to you too, Logan," I said, stretching my arms wide hoping that she didn't sense my uncertainty at the time.

"Oh, good morning. Are you and my daddy boyfriend and girlfriend now? We've never had a step-mama before." I almost choked on the air I was breathing.

"Your dad and I are just friends, okay? You won't be having a step-mother anytime soon, at least not with me." I tried to say it as playfully as I could.

"Okay, well you can come down, lunch is ready. And if you need a toothbrush, there are some in my dad's bathroom." I knew lil' miss thing was not trying to tell me that my breath stank.

I wrapped the blanket around me and headed to the bathroom to handle my hygiene. I wasn't about to put those greasy work clothes back on, so I found one of Game's t-shirts to throw on. As I was walking to the kitchen, I heard Ava going on and on about how she did some kind of family genogram in school.

"I learned that I am 28% Cherokee. Is that on your side or Mom's?" She went on and on about her new discovery.

"Baby I don't know, but probably mine. You see these waves," he joked.

"Good morning," I announced, and everyone looked at me. Game stood at the stove shirtless with a spatula in his hand. He looked at me and smiled before reaching out to me. I walked closer to him reluctantly and he pecked me on my forehead and gave my ass a little squeeze. I tried to put on my bravest face, but I looked back and the girls were all tuned in.

"Anna and Jahfar sitting in the tree, K. I. S. S. I. N. G.," Logan sang out. I swear if I was light skin, my cheeks would have been flushed. Game ignored his daughter and turned his attention to me.

"Girls, Anna is a part of my middle name so you can call me Misty if you'd like." I looked at the both of them for their reaction.

"That is ugly," Ava said, scrunching up her nose.

"Well, I like it. It has a nice ring to it," Logan joked.

"The girls want wings and I'm about to make me a salad. What would you like?" Game pulled me in his direction.

I couldn't even concentrate because of the fine specimen that was standing in front of me. And I also couldn't get last night out of my head.

"Whatever you're eating is cool Jahfar," I said, never making eye contact with him. I'm sure he could sense my awkwardness.

THE REALEST IN THE GAME WANTS HER

I sat down at the table trying to do anything but look in his direction as the girls argued about who looked the most like their dad.

"Girl, you know I look like him the most. I have his skin tone and everything," Logan snapped.

"Skin color doesn't matter little girl. I have his eyes and his nose," Ava countered back.

"Whatever. You were probably adopted!"

"Girls!" Game finally butted in, his tone commanding not only the girls, but me.

"Both of you look like me and your mother. Now I do not want to hear anything else about it. As a matter of fact, go upstairs until the food is done."

"But Daddy," Logan started to protest, but when she realized that her daddy was serious, she marched her behind up the steps.

Now it was just Game and me, and I couldn't hide behind the girls arguing. I sat idly at the table not knowing what to say or how I was supposed to act knowing that I had just had sex with this man whose sister rescued me from being homeless. It just all seemed too good to be true.

Finally, tired of just sitting idly, I walked over to the fridge and grabbed a bottle of water. My throat felt like the desert. Game eased behind me and wrapped his arms around my waist, but I scooted away from him while giving him a nervous smile.

"What's wrong? You've been acting weird since you came down." He finally picked up on my mood.

"Nothing," I lied, sitting back down at the kitchen island.

"You're lying. Are you regretting what happened last night?"

How in the hell did he just read me like that?

"It's not that. I just don't want you to think less of me," I started.

"Less of you? Why would I think less of you?"

He was now standing in front of the stove with his arms folded across his chest.

I played with my hands, unsure of how to say what I was thinking. Game's glare just made me feel like a scolded child.

"Come on Misty, say what you have to say. I wake up thinking that we are good and now you can't even look at me in the eyes. If last night was a mistake to you, just say it. Stop being a little ass girl about it."

His tone was now elevated, and I knew that he was upset. There was just a lot that Game didn't know about me, like the fact that I questioned everything and had been through so much that made me guarded.

"I'm about to get my driver to take you back to K-Spot," he said dismissively, walking past me.

I stood there for a moment, unsure of how to make things right with him. After all, he had been so good to me. Maybe I was overreacting, but that was what I tended to do so that I would have a reason to walk away.

I walked up to Game's bedroom and he was getting dressed. I found my clothing and began to do the same. Game wouldn't even look at me the few times I glanced his way. I had so much that I wanted to say, but I was afraid that he wouldn't understand and would just judge me.

I grabbed the last of my things and turned around to leave, hoping that Game would at least walk me out, but he didn't. He only continued what he was doing, acting like I didn't even exist.

Kayla Gambino

If one more person told me one more thing about Danni, I would snap. It was enough that Fu already had an opinion about her, but now people were coming to my damn job about her. The latest story was that she was stripping at the Cat Trap. I really didn't care about how she chose to live her life just as long as it didn't affect my nieces and nephews.

I drove to her house and didn't see her car or Mario's car in the driveway, but I heard Tae Tae crying from a mile away. I opened the door to clothes all over the ground and a foul odor like someone had died. I raced upstairs to see what was wrong with the baby and he was laying on the bed while my niece I called Stink was sitting crying her tail off. I picked up the baby and rocked him while I sat down with my niece.

"Where is your mommy, Stink?" I asked, but she just kept crying.

"Stinky, where is your mommy?" I asked again.

"Brother, Brother!" she repeated in a high-pitched scream.

Something was wrong and I was starting to panic.

"Where is Trey, baby?" I asked, and she pointed towards the master bedroom. I put Tae Tae down and walked in the bathroom. I let out a gut-wrenching scream as I saw my nephew hanging from the shower rod. There was a sheet attached to the shower rod and it was wrapped around his neck.

"OH MY GOD! BABY YOU WILL BE OKAY!" I said, unwrapping the sheet from his neck. I felt for his pulse, but I couldn't find it. There was no way was I going to let my nephew die. I pulled my phone out and called 9-1-1 and until an ambulance arrived, I gave him chest compressions while Stink and Tae Tae cried to the top of their lungs. Where the hell was Danni? Her kids were all alone and may have witnessed their brother trying to kill himself. Where the fuck was she?

The ambulance arrived ten minutes later, and I was still giving my nephew CPR. The paramedics took over while I went and got the kids. I took the kids away from the chaos and sat them downstairs when I saw a note on the kitchen table with the word *Mommy* written on the front. It read:

Mommy, this is Trey. I love you and my sissys so much, but I am sad. Fixing my sister and brother food, giving them baths and always cleaning up is a lot for me. The kids joke on me in school and call you names. They are really mean. I don't want to hurt your feelings, but I don't want to be hear nemore. Tell Mario I love him, tell nana I will miss her, tell Kayla she is my favorite auntie, and tell Uncle Game that he was the biggest most emportat nice person in the world to me. Bye mama, Trey

I couldn't stop the tears from pouring like a faucet as I closed Trey's last letter. This shit broke my heart that I didn't know he was fighting this internal battle.

"Dammit!" I slammed my hand down on the table. I had to be the one to tell Game. I dropped the kids off at a neighbor's and then drove straight to him. I didn't know why I had to tell him first. Game and Trey had a really special relationship. You would've thought he was his son.

I walked into his house and I could hear laughter coming from the den. He and the girls were down there watching a funny movie all cuddled up. I hated to break them up, but I had to. He noticed my tear-stained face right away.

"What's wrong Kay? Something wrong with Mama?" He jumped up and raced to me.

I shook my head, no, and the tears started to flow again.

"Yo, tell me what's wrong. Who hurt you?!" he yelled.

"It's Trey."

"What about Trey, Kayla?" He was now shaking me, and I could see his eyes about to bulge out of his head.

"I went over to check on the kids and I found him hanging in the bathroom." I tried to say the word hanging a little low because the kids were present. They didn't need to har all of that.

"Hanging? What the fuck you mean hanging?!" he exploded.

I looked at the girls with sympathy, knowing that they would have to find out eventually, but from the look on their faces, they didn't understand what we were saying. "He hung himself Game. Trey is dead," I finally said.

"Man, my fucking nephew is not dead!" he said, pacing around the room.

I noticed Misty walking into the room, and then she said something to the girls briefly while ushering them out of the room. I noticed she had bags in her hands as well, as if she was about to leave. When she came back, she just watched the intensity of the conversation.

"Jahfar, he's gone. I watched them take him away." This was the only time I'd seen my brother break down. He dropped to his knees and cried. I went to console him, but he only pushed me away.

"Get off me man. Don't touch me!" he yelled. I backed up and stood there.

"Jahfar, are you going to come to the hospital? I have to go and tell Mama. I called Danni the whole way over here, but she didn't answer." He didn't even answer, he just balled up on the floor.

"You can go Kayla. I got him," Misty said lowly. I nodded and left to go deliver the news to Mama.

Misty Blue

I kneeled down beside Game and he grabbed on to my waist and held me tightly. He sobbed on me as I rubbed his back. I really didn't deal with these types of things, but I knew his pain. To lose someone so close to you is a tragedy. Those vivid pictures of my slain mom flooded my head. Just minutes before I was about to hop in a Lyft and go back to the K-Spot, I saw Kayla run in, tears flowing down her face. I knew something was wrong, so I decided to put all of the drama in the backseat.

"Irresponsible bitch!" I heard Game curse. "Since she had them kids, she never gave a fuck about them. When I see her, I'ma hurt her ass!"

"Jahfar, I never told you that my mom died. She was assaulted when I was eleven years old and I was there to witness it. I could never remember all the details, but I don't need to. It's painful enough. After my mom died, my dad lost himself. The pain of losing her was too heavy, so he went off and never came back. One day he didn't pick me up from school, and it was the last I saw of him. After that, I didn't have any family here, so I was bounced around from foster home to foster home, ten to be exact. I won't go into too many details about my time there, but it was next to hell. The burns on my back that you saw the other night were from my fourth foster mother who thought that burning my skin with a lighter was purely entertainment.

"I said all of that to say that your sister is going to have a hell of a time accepting the fact that her son is gone. Losing her son is punishment enough. I know it will be hard, but you have to forgive her and be there for her. You don't know how many nights I wished and prayed that someone would've been there for me after my parents died. The people who hurt my mom, I know it haunts them, so I try not to think about it. You have to be there for your sister and help her pull through this."

For the rest of the night we sat in silence and I prayed for this family's healing.

* * *

1 week later

Game and I still hadn't talked about our blow up, partly because he was grieving and partly because I avoided it. I wasn't ready to bare my soul to him, so I tried my best to be there for him and didn't even bring up the argument.

We met at Game's mom's house for the repass. Though the funeral was sad, Trey was sent off beautifully. He had a cobalt blue casket, his favorite color, and dozens of blue moon roses. There was not a dry eye in the church, and I had to stop Game when Trey's father walked in. Big Trey had been an absentee father to his son and daughter since they were born, and he was really abusive to Danni. Game's blood was already boiling with Danni, so he was looking for someone else to take it out on.

Jaylen, Game's older brother, was even in attendance. He was released from prison a day before the funeral after doing two years. I couldn't tell if Game was happy to see him, because the two didn't talk at all. I could see some kind of sibling rivalry going on between them that I would ask about later.

THE REALEST IN THE GAME WANTS HER

Poor Danni couldn't contain herself at the funeral. She howled out loudly as her mom held her. She couldn't even see Trey before he was lowered into the grave, due to her falling out every time she got close to the casket. All in all, it was just a sad day. Danni kept yelling that it was her fault and God should've taken her instead of her son. Her ex, Mario, was in attendance as well. He hung his head low and I could tell he had been close to Trey too. Game, however, was unusually quiet and didn't shed one tear. He paid for the entire funeral and even though he still blamed Danni, he stood by her side the entire time.

Just to make myself busy and avoid the sad family, I got the food out so that everyone could start eating. I felt nervous as hell, so I had to do something to calm my nerves. I just wanted to help. Mario had ordered all the soul food classics from Martins Soul food. I started sitting everything out when Jaylen came in.

"Aye, what's your name again?" I heard him ask.

"It's Misty," I answered, having to mentally correct myself from telling him Anna. I had come clean to everyone about my real name, so there was no need to lie to him.

"You need help with anything?" he asked me. Since he'd gotten out, we were briefly introduced, but hadn't said more than two words to each other after. He was an exact replica of Game; just a little more muscular and with more tats than the subway in Harlem.

"Ummm sure. I'm just putting the food out."

Jalen grabbed the pan of baked spaghetti and put it on the table. People were starting to pile in after coming from the gravesite. I picked up a pan of chicken, but it was so heavy that I nearly dropped it and Jaylen caught it.

"Oh my god, thank you. Do you know how mad folks would've been with me without any chicken to eat?" I laughed.

"Damn right. Ain't no black funeral without any chicken." He laughed.

I grabbed another pan and this one was even heavier with the baked beans. Jaylen noticed me struggling and helped me. Our hands touched just a little when taking the pan, and he gave me a friendly smile. When I looked up, Game was coming into the kitchen.

"Hey. Everything okay?" I said, turning around to grab the other food. I didn't even notice the scowl on his face until I turned back around.

"Aye Jalen, don't touch my fucking girl ever again man," Game said, so calm that it was scary. I didn't even know that I was his girl.

"Man, gone head with that shit!" Jaylen replied.

"Aite, go ahead and try me boy!" Game said, patting his waist, and I saw that he had a gun. I had never seen him carry a gun before.

"Let me speak to you outside for a moment," Game added to me in more of a demanding way than asking me. Before I could even respond to him, he was out the door and I was following.

I walked outside and he was standing with his hands in the pockets of his Balmain slacks.

"What is your problem? And why do you have that at a funeral?" I asked, pointing to his waist.

"I don't ever come out unless I'm strapped baby girl," he said condescendingly, like I was just supposed to know that. "But check this out, I don't want you around my brother."

"Why not?"

"Because I said so. Anything else?" he asked.

I squinted my eyes up at him and frowned before walking back into the house. This was not the place or the time. For the rest of the night I tried my best to avoid him and keep my spirits up.

Back at his place, I was tired of the silent treatment that was going on, so I broke the ice.

THE REALEST IN THE GAME WANTS HER

"So, are you going to tell me what's really going on? I know the death of your nephew is devastating, but that had nothing to do with what happened earlier with your brother."

"I don't even want to discuss that right now. I'm not in the mood. Oh, and you can go anyway. I know you really don't even want to be here. Before my nephew died, you were packing your shit up."

I sighed. "Really? This is how we talk to each other now?"

I hopped my tiny self in front of him. He was really about to walk past me.

"Misty for real, you are testing me right now."

"So, answer my question."

"My brother is just not a good person, aitc?" He finally gave in to me. "That's who Bregan stepped out on me with."

"The girls' mom?" I asked, puzzled, softening my demeanor.

He nodded, yes.

"Damn, you think he would try to make a move on me too? I thought that y'all were trying to work on y'all's relationship."

"Man, that nigga is grimy. I don't care about reconciling nothing with him. When we were younger, I wanted to be like his ass, but he kept getting locked up and I hit the block so I could take care of my family. That was a problem for him. When he came home from Juvie, he was mad that I was out here doing my thing. Jealousy is a mutherfucker, especially when it comes from your family."

I started to say, *at least you have family*, but I kept it to myself.

"Well, don't let that worry you. Don't you have a deadline coming up? That's where your focus needs to be right now," I said, trying to change the subject.

"You're right," he said, pecking me on my lips and then heading for the shower.

I sat on his California King and started to curl up with my new book, *The Hate You Give,* when my phone chimed. It was a text from Chandler saying that she had found me a 2-bedroom townhouse. I nearly jumped up and down for joy. I had been working my ass off at Starbucks for about two months and stacking. I had even filled out an application to get my GED. Things were kind of coming together but I didn't want to jinx it, so I kept moving the same way I did when I was broke. I mean, Starbucks was paying me about $900 every two weeks, and that wasn't a lot, but I had been with Game a lot, so I didn't have to pay for anything. On top of that, I was still getting a few things right for the library, so that would be up and running in a few months. I wanted all African-American authors, so ordering books was taking time.

Game walked out of the shower with a towel around his waist. Baby boy was dripping wet looking all sexy as usual, but before my mind raced to all the nasty things that I wanted to do to him, I had to tell him my good news.

"Jahfar! Guess what!" I said while jumping on the bed excitedly.

He just looked at me like he was not in the mood to play the guessing game.

"Well okay, attitude central. But anyway, my friend found me a place finally! I am happy to finally have my own, my FIRST OWN!" I was smiling from ear-to-ear, but Game did not share my excitement.

"Why are you looking like that?" I asked all out of breath from jumping.

"I just don't get why you were so pressed about finding a place when you could've just stayed here and stacked," he said, drying his back off with a towel.

"Are you not happy for me?" I was taken aback.

He just kept on doing what he was doing without giving me a response.

"This is supposed to be a good thing. I wouldn't depend on you for a place to stay when I'm now in a position to get my own." I looked at him weirdly.

"It's like you have a point to prove or something. There isn't a question of whether you can do it. You are more than capable, but I think it's just dumb, honestly."

"Okay, it's dumb because I'm going out here getting my own, but the thing you say you hated about your baby mama was that she sat around spending your money. Okay, you know what—" I paused. "I'm beginning to think that you and I moved a little too fast. Maybe we need to take a step back," I said, a little sadness in my voice.

I just didn't get his problem and arguing with him was beginning to be draining. Like, every little thing didn't have to be the end of the world. And then he had this attitude as if he was the only one who had a say in this relationship or whatever we were doing. I was starting to think that I should've just kept it moving that day that Kayla came to his house, then I wouldn't be going through this.

"You're not getting what I'm saying, but I'ma just let it be. Congrats on your place and we can do whatever you want to do." He slipped on some boxers and left the room, leaving me standing there not knowing what to say.

"Thanks ASSHOLE!" I yelled. Now I really couldn't wait to get in my own place.

Fuquan Grimes

The shit with Trey had been killing me. It had been a few weeks since his funeral, but the shit felt like it happened yesterday. It was crazy because back when she was pregnant, Danni used to joke and say that I was gone be her baby's god-daddy, but I never took that shit serious. The whole reason that Game and I were friends was because of Danni. She was arguing with her nigga one day and he was acting like he was about to do something stupid, so I intervened and walked her home, and that's how I met Game. He was appreciative of me looking out for his sister and the rest was history.

I hit the florist so I could get her some flowers and a sympathy card since I hadn't seen her since the funeral. I wanted to check on her to see how she was doing since she had always been like a kid sister to me, until recently. She was definitely a little extra the last time I saw her, but I would give her a pass this time.

I knocked on her door a few times but got no answer. Her car was in the driveway, so I turned the knob and it opened. The horror stories were true about the way her house looked, and I couldn't even walk without tripping over a pizza box or something. Mario had gotten her this nice ass townhouse and she wasn't even taking care of it. I maneuvered through the house and saw that the trash was spilling over and shook my head. I was beyond disgusted when I took out the trash and some shit fell on my shoes. I hurriedly took it outside and tried to calm myself down before I went upstairs to see Danni.

I just hated dirty shit and Kayla was so clean, so I didn't know where Danni got the dirty shit from. I walked up the stairs and found it was just as dirty up there as where I had just come from. I was glad that the kids were with Kayla and her mom because they did not need to be in all this filth. Danny laid on the bed with her back facing me and I could hear her sniffling. I walked around to her and she turned over on the other side. I could tell she had been crying and not getting any sleep from the huge black rings around her eyes.

"Danni, I know you're going through it right now and you think shit won't get any better, but it will baby girl. I didn't come here to worry you, but I'ma just sit with you for a little while. We don't even have to talk."

I cleared the seat next to her bed and just sat with her. I couldn't imagine what she was going through. I'd never lost anyone this close to me in my life and I would die behind my baby girl. I thought it was too early for Danni to get over it, but she still had two kids that she had to look after. We couldn't let the same outcome happen with them so I would help her get back to being the person that she once was.

Back in the day, Danni was legit my best friend, outside of her brother. We had become cool with me being at their crib all the time; you know, shit sort of just blossomed with our friendship. I used to talk to her 'bout the janks I was messing with and she had me beating chicks up behind her. What she didn't know was I was feeling Kayla. Back in the day, Kayla was the little geeky girl with glasses who stayed in the house reading books. When she was sixteen I was nineteen, so I wouldn't dare try her, but I had my eye on her, and the older she got, the more she bloomed. Soon, all the niggas in the hood were on her with her lemon-colored skin, petite body and the tiny freckles that were beautifully placed on her face. I ran all them niggas away.

I sat in silence with Danni while she cried softly. I wanted to somehow soothe her and make her pain go away, but I knew that that was not possible. It would be a long road for her, and she would have to forgive herself and learn from her mistakes.

"Why Fu?" I heard her say softly. "Why did MY son have to do that?"

I didn't even know what to say.

"I don't know Dan. He wasn't happy here."

"I will tell you why." She was now sitting up, eyes bulging out of her head, looking at me.

"He did it because he had a selfish ass mama. It was me! You can say it. It was me!" She beat on her chest while saliva flew out of her mouth.

"Come on Danni, don't say that," I started.

"Say what? That my son hanged himself in my motherfucking bathroom? That bathroom right there?" She pointed to the bathroom behind me.

"My baby hanged himself right from that shower rod. How am I supposed to sleep here when my son killed himself five feet away from where I lay my head?"

I just shook my head. I really had no idea of what to say.

"Fu, I just want to feel better!" she cried.

"Things are going to get better Sis. Trust me!"

I walked up to her and took her in my arms like a loving big brother would do. I was used to street shit like shooting niggas and rolling dice, but I was not familiar with this type of stuff. For a moment, I just stood there holding her while she sobbed into my new Givenchy hoodie.

"We gone get through it, Sis."

Danni lifted her head and looked at me before stepping back and dropping down on her knees. At first, I thought she dropped something until she started to tug at my belt. I swatted her hand away so damn fast.

"Yo! Fuck is up wit' you!" I stepped back from her and she looked up at me all childlike. "Don't just look. What did you think you were about to do?"

"I just wanted you to make me feel better."

"Danni, I know you just lost your son, but that is no excuse to be on this bullshit you're on, because you tried this shit before. Tighten up man."

It was like I was speaking to a brick wall or something. She got up and walked up to me trying to grab my face to kiss me.

"Yo, you smoking dope or something? Move before I hurt yo' lil' ass."

I tried not to take the frustration I was feeling out on her, but I still ended up pushing her ass on the bed and walking out.

"Don't say shit else to me either, Danni."

I drove home so taken aback at the way she'd acted and now I had to figure out how I was gone tell this shit to Kayla, or if I would even tell her at all.

Danniece Gambino

"Well, leave then bitch like the rest of them," I yelled to Fu's back. I thought he would turn around, but he never even looked back.

It had been two days since I'd put my baby into the ground, threw dirt on top of him and walked away. I constantly blamed myself for his death, but I also blamed my family. The only person who helped me was my mama. My brothers and sister made it seem like they did so much for my kids when they really didn't. All Game did was throw money at them and Kayla just posted them on Facebook and Snapchat pretending to be the number one Auntie, when in reality, she went months without talking to my kids.

Everyone had been tiptoeing around me, but I knew that they blamed me. Game could barely say two words to me, Kayla gave me these pitiful smiles, my youngest brother tried his best to comfort me, and my mama had my daughter. I think she only took her because she was afraid that something would happen to her too. Mario had had Tae Tae for a little while now and even though he was there for me during the funeral, I'd heard he had a little girlfriend. Fuck him. Fuck everybody. Everyone was supposedly so concerned about me at the funeral, but since then, not one person had reached out. I'd sit in this house in my bed all day, alone.

Fu was the only person to come and see me and I just wanted him to feel for me the way I felt for him. Fu and I had been friends since we were teenagers, and all the while he referred to me as his best friend, never knowing that I wanted more. We would flirt every now and then, but he never took me serious, claiming Game would kill him if he ever touched any one of his sisters. Funny how he dropped that motto. Now, he was fucking my baby sister and he looked at me like I was the shit on the bottom of his shoe.

Didn't he know that my heart hurt so bad after losing Trey? Did anybody know? Every day I thought that I would literally die of a broken heart. My oldest son had been hanging from the shower rod ten feet away from my bed. I couldn't even look in the direction of the bathroom. Every time I tried to turn the knob to go in, I broke down and cried, never opening the door. I hadn't showered since the funeral and I didn't plan to. There was no need. Mario didn't want me, Fu didn't want me, none of my kids were with me, nothing was going right for me, and a couple of times I questioned whether I should just go ahead and be with Trey. How would I get by without my oldest born? We grew up together. I didn't know shit about being a mom when I had him, so as I was teaching him, he was teaching me.

"LORD WHY?!" I hollered. My voice echoed against the vibrations of the wall. "Why did you take my fucking baby?"

I rose from the bed and walked towards my baby's room. I came here about three times a day, each time walking away before I got into the room. Today would be the day that I would actually go in. I needed to be closer to my baby. I turned the doorknob, slowly taking a deep breath before the door finally opened. The whiff of crayons and glue hit my nose instantly and I melted. Trey's room was just like it was the day that he died. His cobalt blue comforter was thrown lazily across his bed, and his Nintendo controllers were on the floor so I went to pick them up. I'd told this boy a million times not to leave his things on the floor. I'd paid a pretty penny for this damn game.

I couldn't help but smile to myself remembering how mad Trey would get whenever his sister bothered his things. She was never allowed in his room, so if anything was out of order, he knew that she had been the culprit. My smile slowly faded and tears instantly began to fall. I would never hear my babies fussing again. I curled up in his bed hugging his pillow tight. With time, I hoped that I would come to terms with what happened to my son and the role that I played in what happened. Today would be hard, and the day after that, and maybe even a month after that. It would just be me and my memories and things that I wished I had done differently. Most of all, I wished that I would have made Trey his pancakes.

Misty Blue

I woke up clawing at my throat in a sweat drenched t-shirt. I was so thirsty that it felt like I hadn't drunk anything in days. I knew it came from me yelling from the constant nightmares that I had been having. I reached beside me and grabbed the bottle that was half-full and gulped the water all the way down in a matter of seconds.

Tonight, the nightmare was the same as it had been for the past couple of nights; I was basically reliving the night my mother was killed. These nightmares were so vivid that it seemed like the entire scene was tattooed in my mind. I mean, I could smell and taste everything that I did that night and the shit scared the hell out of me like it had all those years ago.

I thought about calling Game to confide in him, but I knew I couldn't do that. We moved very fast, and to be honest, I didn't need that distraction in my like. It seemed like being with him made me happy, but at the same time, everything that he was going through was causing me to relive my past; a past that I'd shielded myself from for so long.

It had been three days since I last heard from him and I was avoiding him like the plague. I was complicated and from what I could see, he was too, and that just made for a disaster. I had to get myself together and focus on me. Chandler had found me a place, I had a job, and that was all that I needed to be worried about.

I'd also made the decision that I would give Game back the deed to the library that he purchased for me. I just didn't need to feel like I was indebted to him because I honestly needed to detach myself from him. Sure, Kayla and I would always be cool for everything that she had done for me, but I knew that I could no longer burden her or Game. I had to put my big girl panties on and finally do something for myself, on my own.

I fell asleep about an hour later and had to be right back up to get ready for work in three hours. I knew that today would be a long day and I prayed that it flew by. The faster it went by, the quicker I could make it to Game's home to give him back the deed to the library.

I walked up to his home, kind of nervous about what I was about to do, but I knew that it had to be done. That was stupid of me to accept such a large gift from a man anyway. No one had ever given me anything except Mama C, and she taught me the value of hard work. I hadn't done anything to get this library, so rightfully, it didn't belong to me.

I sat the deed to the library on the porch and started to scurry away when the door was swung open.

"DADDYYY, your little friend is here," a rude Ava said and then skipped right on past me.

This little thing had blown my cover. My plan was to just leave the deed and I wouldn't have had to even see Game, but now he was standing in the doorway with Logan by his side staring right at me.

He picked up the deed from the ground and after realizing what it was, he shook his head.

"You want to come in and talk?" he asked.

I so badly wanted to say no, but when this man spoke it was like he cast a spell over me, so I reluctantly followed him.

Logan went off into another room, leaving Game and me alone to talk.

"Running again, I see," he spoke calmly.

"I'm not running. I'm here in your presence, aren't I?" I replied, finding my strength.

"So, why did you bring me this?" He flung the papers across the room.

"Because I shouldn't have accepted it in the first place. Please believe that I am grateful for everything but—"

"But what? This is the way you show your gratitude? By returning the gift?"

"Look, I didn't come here to do this with you. Thank you for everything, but you and I are just too different. We would never be able to work."

I turned around to walk away.

"What if I needed you?" I heard him say, prompting me to turn around.

"What?"

"What if I need you? I don't know what you are doing to me Misty, but I need you. You say that crystal that you wear around your neck brings you peace, well you are my peace," he said sincerely.

"You don't need me, and I don't have anything to give you. Don't you see that I am broken and empty? Empty with nothing to give."

I clutched my heart as I wiped away the falling tears. I didn't want to admit it, but since I'd met Game he had been my peace as well, even when we were arguing. I was just scared and didn't want to rush things with him. I was scared that he would see me for the broken girl that I was.

"Blue, I don't see broken. I see a fighter. I see a beautiful woman with scars who is deserving of love just like anyone else. I see the woman that I want to take a chance on."

"Game, I don't know," I said, still wiping away tears. I would punch my damn self in the throat if I cried in front of this man.

"You don't have to know. Let's just do this shit." He put it simply.

After staring at him for a moment, I finally nodded, indicating that I would give this crazy love a chance.

"Yeah, let's do this shit!" I heard from behind me, and there stood Logan which made me bust out laughing. This little girl was mess.

"Grounded! Two weeks!" Game yelled.

Game Gambino

Misty and I had just come from getting furniture for her new place. This girl had me out for hours asking me about color schemes and shit, like I could really help her out. She really needed some girlfriends. Once Misty finished her house shopping, we were on our way to dinner when I got a call from my ex, Bregan.

"Hello Game. You better come get your damn daughter before I snap her neck. She's getting too damn grown!" she hollered, causing Misty to cock her neck at me.

"Calm down, Bre. I can't understand nothing you're saying with all of that hollering. And don't threaten my kid."

"Oh, shut up Game and come and get her. The back talk and sassy ways are getting to be too much for me right now. You know I did this shit for you anyway."

"Did what shit?" I asked confused.

"You know. Don't act stupid."

I ignored whatever bullshit she was hinting at.

"Man, quit going around the shit and tell me exactly what she did."

"I told her to make sure she picked her sister up from the afterschool bus, but instead, she decided to go hang out at her friend Shannon's house. Ava stayed at school 'til damn near 7 pm because the bus had to take her back and your phone went straight to voicemail. Then when I confronted her about it, she said it's not her job and one of her parents needs to do it. I'm telling you come get your daughter."

"Aite, Bre. I'm on my way. Be there in a few," I answered and then hung up.

As much as Bregan and I didn't get along, I wouldn't stand for either of my kids disrespecting her. That was just something they wouldn't do.

"What was that all about?" Misty asked.

"Man, Ava smelling her ass," I replied.

"Hmm, teenagers for you," she replied.

I was at Bregan's place in less than ten minutes, and as soon as I pulled up, Ava was flying out of the house with major attitude, getting in the car and slamming the door. I turned and looked at her like she had lost her mind.

"Hi Daddy. Hi Misty," she said with her stubborn ass.

I didn't lay into her in the car, but once we got home, I didn't waste any time.

"What's up Ava? Tell me your side now that I've heard what your mom had to say."

"Dad, she's so unfair and makes me babysit all of the time. I can't even hang out with my friends." She pouted.

"So, you're telling me that your mom asked you to do something and you defied her just because?"

"But Daddy," she started. I had given her an opportunity to plead her case and she basically told me the short version of what her mom said.

"Baby you can't not listen to your mom. I know you thought that coming here would be you getting off, but I can't do that this time. You are on punishment for the next two weeks. Straight to school and back here. I will pick you up every day. Now give me your phone."

"Really Dad? You're just going to take her side like that?"

"Yep, just like that."

I held my hand out for her phone and she dropped it and went running to her room.

"I hate my life," she screamed like those little white girls on tv.

"You will get over it."

"Whoa. So I'm guessing that didn't go well." Misty came down from her shower.

"She just whizzed past me so fast that I didn't even know who she was."

"Yeah. I ain't stunting her ass," I replied.

"Yeah, yeah, whatever punishment you gave her will be over in two days. You know that you are a softie, especially when it comes to Ava."

"Yeah, I'm like that with both of my girls, but not this time."

"No. You love both of them, but you have a different kind of vibe with Ava," I peeped.

"Oh yeah? Well let me peep you," I asked, eyeing her up and down. She was still towel drying her hair and she wore a half crop top with her titties hanging out just a little with black leggings.

"Oh, no you don't." She caught my drift.

"Not while your teenage daughter is here," she said, scooting away from me.

"Huh? She's gone be here for two weeks. You're telling me I have to wait two weeks? You're at work when she's at school."

"I guess so," she said playfully, twerking her butt in the air. But her ass couldn't get away from me that fast. I caught her by her elbow as she was walking away and propped her on the bathroom counter.

"Wait baby," she started, but shut up as soon as I entered her. "Baby, stop," she lustfully moaned in my ear, but I only inched deeper and deeper into her. "Oh baby, you're so big. Don't do this to me," she said, and then started biting my shoulder. I had to laugh at the shit that she was saying because she came up with some new shit every time.

"It's too big? You want me to stop?" I asked, pumping in and out of her, holding her waist.

"Uhhh, no!" she whined until we both climaxed, and she collapsed in my arms. "Oh my god," she said breathlessly. "I hope she didn't hear us. Why did you do that?" She punched me in the chest with her little fist and it felt like a little pinch.

"Girl, she didn't hear us. She's probably up there with her headphones on, writing a fuck you status to me on Facebook."

"She will be okay. I wish I still had a father to scold me," she said solemnly.

That shit hit me once again because I knew that I was the cause of it. Each time I built up my courage to tell her that I was one of the ones who broke in her house, I just couldn't. My love was getting so deep for her and she was doing so well that I didn't want to bring her back down. The shit killed me.

"Babe, I have to tell you about something," I said lowly.

"Okay babe," she said, while pecking my chest. "Let's take a shower first."

THE REALEST IN THE GAME WANTS HER

She grabbed my hand and led me to the shower, and this was another opportunity for me to say something, but I didn't.

Misty Blue

I woke up bright and early to make breakfast as King Jahfar had requested the night before. He claimed that I never cooked and all I did was work, so today on my off day, I would stay home and do nothing with him. I did the absolute most cooking; eggs, bacon, sausage, waffles, french toast, frittatas, and fried potatoes with freshly squeezed orange juice. I could tell he was impressed by the huge smile he bore on his goofy face.

"I know, I know," I boasted as Game came up behind me and placed delicate kisses on my face and neck.

"Breakfast first, then you," he joked.

I made him and Ava a plate, but as we started to eat, she hadn't come down yet.

"Is Ava eating?" I asked, while he was stuffing his face with potatoes. I was surprised he even requested breakfast because everyone knew he was a health nut.

"AVAAAAA? GET YOUR BUTT DOWN HERE AND EAT!" he screamed from the table.

THE REALEST IN THE GAME WANTS HER

After two minutes, she still hadn't come down and I could tell Game was getting a little frustrated.

"Let me get this one, Hulk," I said as I got up from the table and headed to her room.

Once I got there she was still laid out in bed, not even dressed for school.

"Hey. Can I talk to you?" I asked, but she didn't respond, and I saw the air pods in her ears. I tapped her lightly and she took them out.

"So, I know you don't want to hear all of this but I'm going to say it anyway." I sat across from her at the computer chair.

"I know things are hectic with school, boys, chores and just being a teenager, but I've been through it too, so I know how it goes. I'm not here to be your mom or lecture you, but I just want to ask you to give me a chance. I don't know you well and you don't know me, but I would like to try to form some type of relationship, even if it's just saying hi and bye. I'm a really nice person, and who knows, we may have some things in common. So, what do you say? Can we start over and get to know each other? After that, if you don't like me, you can do away with me, but at least give it a chance."

I sat there pleading with her with my eyes and for a moment, she only looked at me. I held my breath hoping that she would be down with what I was saying.

"Okay," she said lowly, forming what resembled a smile before getting up to hug me.

"Now come on and get dressed so you can get some of all that food I cooked before your father eats it all."

"Yeah. You know he's greedy," she said while laughing.

When she came down, surprisingly, she kissed Game on the cheek and sat down to eat. Game smiled at me like I had worked a miracle or something, and I playfully dusted my shoulders off.

Ava went off to school, and Game's promise to stay in with me all day proved to be hard for him to keep. Out of nowhere, he said something about needing to head to the office to get something. Now I wasn't the jealous type, but him hopping up and leaving seemed strange. I mean, Game was the man in the streets so I was sure he had bitches at his beck and call. I wasn't sure if he could turn down the amount of pussy that was being thrown at him daily, and that scared me. We hadn't set in stone that we were in a relationship, but I thought that it was understood. I prayed that he wasn't the type of man who wanted his cake and ate it too. The shit bugged the hell out of me until I drifted off to sleep.

I sat on what the hoes called the boulevard for hours with my stomach grumbling, but I was determined not to ask anyone for any money like I usually saw the panhandlers do. It was the summer after I'd left my last foster home and I wasn't going back. I would kill myself first.

"Hey girl," my new friend Ronnie said. She was dressed in a tiny red, leather, mini-skirt and a tank top showing all her jelly rolls. It was 90 degrees out and she was showing out.

"I'm about to find a trick so I can get us some McDonald's tonight."

Ronnie was a little up there in age, so she couldn't stand a chance with the young girls that sold pussy. Ronnie would trick for everything from cigarettes to beer to McDonald's. She quickly disappeared into the summer night as a baby blue-colored Lincoln came, and she hopped in the car.

I sat and watched girl after girl get into various cars; some nice while the others were old and frumpy looking. My hunger pains didn't subside and now it literally felt like I would pass out. I had to do something, so when the Lexus truck pulled up, and I heard the man whistle at me, I talked myself into getting money to feed myself for the night. I was seventeen and I had been on the streets for damn near a year and still didn't have so much as a pair of drawers to my name.

I slowly walked to the car while trying to smooth my hair out. I got in and the cool air immediately made my nipples harden. John B, I called him, really liked that.

"What's your rate for some head?" he asked. I didn't know what the hell he was talking about but before he could change his mind, I spit a number out.

"$100."

He drove to an abandoned park and stopped the car.

"Well, get to it," he said, pointing to his semi-erect dick.

I really didn't know how to give a man oral because I had never done it before. I slowly lowered my head down and opened my mouth, and he shoved my head down causing his tiny penis to not even get further than the middle of my tongue. He jerked my head back and forth until tears came to my eyes and I felt like I would throw up nothing all over him. He was having a good ole time too, because I heard him sounding like a dog in heat. I tried to remove his hand from my head, but he was too strong.

The embarrassment lasted for nearly twenty minutes before he finally came in my mouth. I hopped out of the car so fast to spit that shit out that you would have thought my ass was on fire. Without saying a word, he threw a $20 bill out of the window at me and sped off. I was so hurt, but what did I expect when doing this kind of thing? I wanted to cry all night, but I couldn't because that scum wasn't worth my tears. I walked back to my spot, all the while thinking at least Ronnie and I would have food tonight.

THE DOOR SLAMMING WOKE me up out of my sleep and when I looked at the alarm clock, it was 2 am. Game had left out of the house around three saying that he would be right back, but it took him almost twelve hours to get back really quick, as he put it. I was pissed off and he was going to know it. He walked in and went straight to the shower. Weird.

He came out fifteen minutes later, smiling like the Dove man soap. He noticed that I was up and came towards me.

"You still up?" he asked, coming to kiss me, but I turned my head.

"What's wrong with you? As a matter fact, I don't even want to know," he said, walking away and going over to get some clothes.

"We've been doing good for almost forty-eight hours."

"Where did you go today?" I asked. It was like the calm before the storm.

"Handling business," he said quickly like he didn't owe me anything else.

"Are you irritated or something? Because you shouldn't be. I'm the one who was in the house all day alone!"

"Don't complain when you're in a mansion, Misty," he said cockily. It was just like a man to throw material things in your face.

"Please. Let's not be funny," I said, launching a pillow at him.

"Nah, you stop playing and go to bed. Trying to start an argument for nothing. I don't do too much arguing."

I chuckled. "It's not nothing!" I got up from the bed. "If I was out all day, didn't call or pick up the damn phone, I'm sure it would be a problem, so stop trying to make light of the way I feel."

I tried to hold back the tears that were threatening to fall. I was a punk. I'd had men boss me around and not listen to me all my life, and I didn't want to feel that way in my relationship.

"Misty, I'm a grown ass man. I don't have to check in with you. If I didn't call, it meant that I was busy."

I couldn't take how nonchalant he was acting. I was trying to be an adult about it, but he was making it very difficult for me.

THE REALEST IN THE GAME WANTS HER

"You know what? Fuck you Jahfar!" I yelled, and I rarely cursed or yelled.

"Yeah, do that instead of all this bullshit ass arguing."

I got back in the bed and turned my back to him and decided to just go to sleep. I wouldn't press the issue any further, but I would act accordingly. I was used to disappointment anyway and I was finally learning that no man would treat me the way my father did.

Game laid down finally and I made sure that he wasn't touching me. Childish, I know, but I didn't want to be bothered with someone who stomped on my feelings. Each time he would ease on my side I would move further and further away until I was almost on the ground.

"Blue, I know this is a California King, but it's only so far that you can go to get away from me," I heard him say, but I didn't reply.

"Blue, let's talk," I heard him say while reaching over to touch me.

"Oh, now you want to talk? Well I don't." I swatted his hand away and I could feel him seething. He didn't like it when the shit was done to him.

Just when I was getting to sleep well, the light was turned on and the covers were being flung off me. I looked up to see Game standing over me.

"Oh my god," I said, putting the pillow over my face, but that was snatched too.

"Yo' ass is not going to sleep so you might as well get up and talk to me," Game said seriously.

"You are impossible," I said, finally sitting up and facing him.

"You gone talk or what? I'm not with the attitude."

"Whaaaaaattt?" I laughed. "Me, with my attitude, tried to talk earlier but you wanted to talk about me sitting up in a mansion. Grow up Jahfar!" I threw one of his lines at him. "You left here at 3 pm and didn't get back until 2 am and you expect me not to question you about it?" I tilted my head to the side like that would make him understand better.

"You were asking me about where I was for a reason, so ask exactly what you want to know instead of going around it. You know I hate when you do that Blue." He kept calling me by my last name, irritating me even more.

"Okay." I shrugged. "Are you and I monogamous? I didn't think that this was a conversation that we needed to have, but I guess we do."

Game only laughed and dropped his head. "Again, ask me what you want to know because that definitely is not it. Ask me am I out here fucking other bitches and where I was today because you just assumed that that's what I was doing," he spat.

"Well," I said, waiting for him to answer his own question.

"You're the only one on my radar, Blue. When I let you into my home with my kids and chased your ass down, I thought you knew that. I have not been with anyone but you and don't want to."

He then got into the bed and attempted to go to sleep.

Now I felt kind of bad for accusing him but then another part of me was like, *girl you're good.* He should've just answered me when I tried to talk to him the first time. Now he was mad and I was up looking crazy with no sleep in me. I scooted a little closer to him and wrapped my arms around him.

"Get the fuck off me Misty," he said harshly, but that didn't deter me. We never went to sleep angry.

"Honeeeeyyy," I cooed his name. "I'm sorry for accusing you but you could've called."

"Aite. You're good," he said, but I knew he was still upset. There was only one thing that I could do to really apologize.

I slid down under the covers and stopped right at the little peek-a-book part of his boxers. I didn't know why he was still acting like he was mad when his dick was hard just at the touch. I placed sloppy kisses all up and down his shaft before taking him into my mouth. Before he knew it, I devoured his dick whole, making him shake a little. His dick hitting the back of my throat while I played with his balls was the best part. I bobbed my head up and down slowly while massaging his balls with my hand. His hands palmed my head as I bobbed faster and faster.

"Nasty girl," I heard him moan, which signaled me to keep on going, making his toes curl. The sounds of my gags filled the room and I was happy that Ava's room was on the opposite end of the hall. I let his balls go and stroked his dick in a twisting motion with one of my hands while still sucking it. This made him go crazy pushing my head so far down that I thought his dick would go through my stomach. Dumping all his kids inside of me, I drank it slowly before sitting up and facing him. He couldn't still be mad.

I stroked him back to life before sliding on him nice and easy. I locked eyes with him and he fondled my nipples, causing me to moan out.

"UHHH, JAHFARR!"

I rode him insanely while not taking my eyes off him. We were locked in now and forever in many ways that he didn't even know yet. Game grabbed my hips and lifted me up and down on his dick, and our bodies mashing together made a popping sound. The feeling was intense but pleasurable at the same time.

"You gone question me again?" I heard him say, but by now I was in my own world. A slap to my ass brought me back to him.

"Huh, you gone question me again?"

"NOOO," I breathlessly said. "I won't. I will be good."

We continuously smashed into one another until we both crashed, cumming together.

"We good?" Game asked, while holding me under the sheets.

"Yeah, we are. I didn't mean to be so extra today, if that's how you took it, but I know I'm not the best and there are girls lined up to get with you every day."

"But I don't want them, Blue. Never did. That's what you have to accept on your own because I can't make you. I want the person I'm with right now. I get what you were saying though; I could've called you just so you wouldn't have to worry."

That statement made me more assured in my relationship and I couldn't say never, but I would try not to accuse him again. His ass had better not ignore my concerns again.

Kayla Gambino

I paced back and forth in my room while Fu played the game downstairs. I didn't want to seem like the jealous girlfriend but while he was gone, he left his phone and I checked it. I wasn't expecting to find anything but was just pressing my luck. Everything was cool until I saw texts from this unsaved number. Whoever it was had texted him damn near twenty times, and even though he didn't respond back, it was a little suspect to me.

I tried calling the number back but whoever it was must've had a burner phone or something because I couldn't call it back. This crap was really scaring me because I had never loved a man like I loved Fu before, and I couldn't chance him cheating on me. When I was young, I watched my mom get stepped on by man after man and I promised myself that wouldn't be my life.

I heard Fu coming up the stairs, but that didn't calm me.

"Yo, what's going on with you? You got something to ask me or something? You only pace like that when you got some shit on your mind." Fu could see right through me so I could no longer hide it.

"Well, I didn't do this to be nosey or anything, but I went through your phone," I said quickly.

Fu shook his head and chuckled.

"And how did that go for you?"

"Well, I found some shit if that's what you're asking. Who is that 228 number that keeps calling and texting you? And don't lie."

"Fuck do I have to lie to you for? But when I tell you, you better be ready for this shit, and don't blame me."

I fell back on the bed bracing myself for whatever news he was about to deliver to me. I could only take so much but I hoped he didn't have some chick knocked up or something when I was two months pregnant and he didn't even know.

"Just tell me, Fu," I said.

"Man, it's your crazy ass sister. She's been stalking me since Trey died."

"What? Get the fuck out of here. Out of all the shit that you could say, you blame my sister?"

"Kay, it's true. I ain't never bite because I love you, but she been doing this shit for a minute now and I have proof."

"So why are you just now telling me if it's been happening?"

"To be honest bae, I thought that she would stop, and I didn't want to have to put you in a position where you would have to choose between me and your sister."

Without a second thought or another word, I got my ass up and flew to my car. I didn't know where Fu thought I was going, but he couldn't catch me fast enough because by the time he got outside, I was pulling off.

My mama's house was twenty minutes away from my house, but I made it to her in ten. Today was Sunday dinner so I knew that Danni would be there. It had been a few weeks since Trey had killed himself, so a part of me didn't want to approach her knowing that she was going through so much, but the other part of me that was racing up to my mother's house told me to fuck her up. I entered the house and as usual, it was packed with family. I spotted her lil' thick ass sitting in the kitchen with my mother and aunts, but I didn't really give a fuck that I was about to blast her in front of my elders. She deserved it.

"You nasty bitch," I stated, hot as hell, while everyone looked at me like I was losing my mind. "Don't sit there and look stupid now. I know what the fuck you've been doing!"

My mom looked like she wanted to slap the shit out of me, but today wouldn't be the right day to try me.

"Kayla, what is all this about? You stormed in here like somebody stole your man or something."

Her choice of words. How ironic.

"Well, this raggedy bitch right here tried to. Why don't you tell Mama what you been doing Danni. Tell her how you tried to fuck Fu even though you know we are together."

My mom gasped, looking at Danni hoping it wasn't true.

"Look Kay, I can explain. I was in a vulnerable place with what happened to Trey," she said sadly.

"Girl, do I look like boo boo the fool to you? I know that you were trying to get with him when you weren't paying no damn attention to your son when he was still here. Don't try to gain the sympathy card here." I busted her simple ass bubble.

"Girl, you're coming in here confronting me when your man was in it too. He wanted me just as bad as I tried him and he never said no," she lied.

"I knew you would try that shit, but I already saw the numerous times you called and he didn't answer and all the unanswered texts you sent. Just be a woman about it and admit your shiesty ass ways hoe!" I guess she was tired of all the name calling and she jumped up in my face.

"Bitch, everyone knew I liked Fu first and you got with him anyway, so I'm not mad at shit I did."

"Girl, who is everybody? You and Fu were friends while your ass was pregnant three times by two different men. No one is scared of you. You may be bigger than me, but size doesn't matter when it comes to these hands."

By now, everyone was trying to pile into the kitchen watching the shit that was about to go down.

"Y'all need to cut this mess out! Y'all are sisters and shouldn't let anyone, let alone a man, come between y'all," my mom tried intervening.

"Mom, this is beyond family. Your daughter here was fully prepared to sleep with my dude just to get back at me for something that I didn't even know I did."

I was so angry to the point that I felt the tears about to slip out.

"So now, we have to get a fair one in. I'm not doing any more talking," I said, pulling my faux locs up into a bun.

"Girl, no one is about to fight your little ass for real. Go back to sucking Fu's dick and we can act like this never happened."

Danni was so loud running her dick suckers that I didn't even know how quiet it had gotten. My family members were no longer cracking jokes and making bets about who would win. I turned around to see Game walking in and it was like everyone knew to straighten the fuck up.

"Fuck is going on in here?" he asked calmly. "I know y'all not in here disrespecting my mama's house. Y'all must have lost y'all minds."

THE REALEST IN THE GAME WANTS HER

You know I was pretty fed up with everyone looking past what the fuck Danni did. Here Game was mad over this bullshit when his drag ass sister was the cause of it.

"All y'all got me fucked up," I said to no one in particular, but every damn body. Game grabbed my arm so hard that I thought that he would break it, and ushered my ass right outside.

"I'ma get you bitch," I said to Danni before leaving. "Yo, get off me," I said to Game when we were finally outside.

"Listen K, I'ma let you slide for now, but the slick shit ain't gone fly for too much longer. Hell is up with you?"

I didn't say anything.

"Speak nigga! It's your time to talk now," he said when I stood there saying nothing.

"Yo' burnt out ass sister tried to sleep with Fu after all the shit I did for her and them damn kids." I felt myself getting hot again.

"And that was enough for you to disrespect my mama's crib like that?"

"So listen, right now I'm not trying to hear all of that. You're clearly not getting where I'm coming from."

"What? Are you slow or something? You do remember Jaylen slept with Bregan, the mother of my kids, and the love of my life. That shit ate me up inside, but I played that shit how it go and caught his ass slipping. And it damn sure wasn't at my mama's crib. So, you know I get your pain, but you got to think smarter and be respectful, or I will whip your ass."

Damn, I wasn't even thinking that Game had been through the same thing as me, but it was worse because he had two kids by the bitch. To this day, I couldn't stand her, and she and Danni were best friends.

"I'm sorry bro. I'ma apologize to Mama and buy her a nice expensive bag," I joked, kind of lightening the mood. Game laughed too and grabbed me for a hug.

"Don't let that shit happen again, kid."

Just as we finished up our conversation, I saw Fu speeding up like a bat out of hell. Too bad he missed all the action. I just got in the car with him, forgetting that I had driven my own car here and not even bothering to explain shit until we got home.

Misty Blue

"Kayla, are you sure you want to do this?" I asked as I held her in the car in front of Planned Parenthood. Kayla decided that after all the shit that went down with her sister and Fu that she wanted to get an abortion. It had been two days since she confronted her sister and it seemed like that was enough time for her to consider getting rid of the baby.

"Yes, I'm sure. I've been going back and forth in my mind about this shit. I prayed on it and this is what I have to do. I'm stressed as hell and I don't want to put a baby through that. I know my sister was being a sneaky bitch, but I'm mad at Fu for keeping the shit from me. I haven't been speaking to him and I'm just not in the right mind to be pregnant right now," she said, psyching herself up. I would support her no matter what she did.

We walked into the building to get the procedure done and it was over before it started. Just that fast, Kay's baby was sucked out of her and she was no longer pregnant. She put on a brave face, but I knew that she was hurting inside, and I would be there for her.

"Can we go to Walmart?" she asked me. I was driving one of Game's cars, so I really didn't care.

"Kay, are you sure you're up to that right now? I mean, you did just have an abortion."

"Girl, I'm fine. I need to go get some snacks and pads since I'ma be in the house for the next few days."

"Okay," I answered, and we made our way to Wally World.

"Girl, I will tell my brother to keep you in the house from now on. Every guy we walk past is all in your ass," Kay said to me.

"Girl please. That's you," I joked.

"No boo, I have on sweats and a t-shirt while you have that waist-length hair down looking cute."

I only had on a leather mini-skirt, a black off-the-shoulder body suit and black chunky heel boots. It wasn't that deep.

"Yep, making a mental note to tell my brother. Make-up on fleek and all of that."

Just as Kayla was bragging on how good I looked, some dude came up offering to pay for our stuff. We only had a few things, so we didn't need him, but Kayla's ass couldn't resist.

"Hell yeah," she said, and the man took out a couple hundred-dollar bills. I literally just stood there while he kept looking at me.

"Can I get your number?" he finally asked. He wasn't bad looking at all, but I wanted no parts.

"Umm no, but she can take yours," Kayla said, taking my phone and entering his name and number.

When he walked away, I fried her ass.

"Yo, why did you just do that? And now my phone is dead, so I can't even delete the shit," I fussed.

"Girl, it will be okay. We had to give him something for paying for this shit. Delete that shit when your phone charges back up."

She thought she was so funny, but I didn't. I hurried up and dropped her ass off and made it to Game's house. I had been gone for hours, so I hoped he wouldn't be home.

I walked in and heard loud music coming from Ava's room and cartoons coming from the other room. I just wanted to lay down and take these hurting ass boots off before my 6 am shift in the morning. I didn't want to argue with Game tonight but something he'd done a few days ago was really bothering me. Well, something he said. I walked in his room and he wasn't there, so I guessed he was in his study working on another game. I showered quickly and as I was coming out, he was coming into the room.

"When'd you get home?" he asked.

"Hey to you too. A little while ago," I said, perked up. We hadn't seen each other all day.

"Where you been?"

"Hanging out with Kayla." I was horrible at lying, but I had to keep Kayla's secret.

"Me and Fu was calling y'all all day and neither one of you answered. Y'all was out thotting or something?"

"If you call a movie and lunch thotting, I guess so."

"What did y'all go see?"

"Dang! What is this? Twenty-one questions?" I asked playfully.

"Hell yeah, so answer them," he snapped.

"How about you answer my question. I overheard you talking to Kayla the other day and you referred to Bregan as the love of your life, like presently, still. What's up with that?"

"Man, you know what I meant. You know I don't even fuck with her like that!"

"The other day it surely didn't sound like that. There was a lot of pain in your voice when you said it."

"So, because you perceived some shit that I said wrong, you and my sister want to keep secrets today?"

He was now back on my whereabouts today and I couldn't keep up with the lies. Damn, me and Kayla should've gone over this shit better.

"Jahfar, I've answered you already," I said, moving around the room so that I could find some lounge wear.

"Bruh, you are insulting my intelligence and I'm about to lose my cool."

He went over to where my phone was charging and pulled it from the plug.

"Put your passcode in."

Dammit, I hadn't even deleted that guy's number.

"Oh, so now we're checking phones?"

I tried to distract him. Damn I was about to get me and Kayla caught if he went through our messages.

"What are you looking for?" I asked before handing my phone over.

Without a word, he sat down on the bed and went through the phone and shook his head. Shit, he had found something.

"This shit ain't none of my business, but how could you go with my sister to do that?"

"Because that's what she wanted to do and she needed support."

"So, this is the reason why neither of y'all could be reached today, because y'all was out getting a fucking abortion. Did you get one too?" he asked sarcastically.

"I'm not pregnant but if I was, it would be an option," I countered.

"Females so damn sneaky, it doesn't make any sense."

Just as he was about to pass me my phone back, a text came through which caused him to shake his head again.

"Kay just text you. She said don't forget to delete that number. What number? I'ma give you a chance to be honest or I can just text back pretending to be you."

Today was just not my fucking day. I slid on a cami and leggings and pondered on if I would rather come clean or get caught.

"Well, we went to Walmart today and some guy asked to pay for our stuff. We let him, and he asked for my number. Kayla then snatched my phone and put his number in it instead, but I didn't plan on calling him or anything," I said all in one breath. I had to throw Kayla under the bus this time.

"So, that's cool? Lying about where you been all day and then getting nigga's number in Walmart. I know yo' Starbucks check ain't but so big, but you needed him to pay for your shit that bad?" Game was throwing some low blows, but I would take them for now.

"It's not what you think babe. It's really all innocent."

I couldn't think of any other way to defend myself.

"Man, fuck that. If the same thing would've happened to me, I don't think you would be so calm. Then you went out in that bullshit," he said, pointing to the mini-skirt that was now in the laundry basket. I wasn't about to go all night with him, so I simply walked away to the guest bedroom and five minutes later, he followed me.

"Bruh, you can walk away all you want, but we gone talk about this shit." He slammed the door and I'm pretty sure the girls heard the sound vibrations.

"Jahfar, what do you want me to say? I didn't do anything wrong. I'm sorry for not being honest with you," I said, sincerely. "Maybe I should just go." I tried walking past him.

"Man, you are not about to do that and play victim here. How am I supposed to believe that you weren't gone call the nigga?" He was fuming.

"Because, I'm with you, STUPID! That's why. I told you the truth and that should be that, but you want to go on and on about nothing."

"'Cause you're foul, yo. I did all this shit to help you and now look how you're acting."

I shook my head. "See, I told you, you only had one time to throw any of the shit you did for me in my face and that would be it." I stormed past him to the bedroom to get my things. I was not staying with him tonight.

I slipped on my slides and started putting my things in my bag when he knocked everything out of my arms.

"Fuck you think this is? You're not leaving here this time of night."

"Yes, I am. I don't want to be in your space right now. You are clearly angry, and it is scaring me. All you will do is throw it in my face later."

Once again, we were arguing for the hundredth time.

I brushed past him and he grabbed my arm firmly and pushed me down.

"Stop trying me Blue. I'm trying to talk to you and walking away when I'm talking is being disrespectful."

"You're not talking to me. You're talking at me and accusing me of stuff. I don't want to do this while the girls are here, and you are scaring me."

I had been hit more than enough times to know that men loved to use their fists when they were angry.

"Man, fuck all of that. Call that nigga!" he yelled, frightening me. I grabbed the phone and looked for a contact that I didn't recognize and there was a contact name Dee. I dialed the number and put it on speaker, but he didn't answer. I called again and still there was no answer.

"See, now what?" I asked.

"Man, I have to go get some air before I lose my mind up in this bitch," he said.

I didn't know why I always ended up feeling bad when I didn't do shit wrong. Game went outside for about fifteen minutes and came back in wearing the same scowl. I knew he wouldn't trust me anymore. He laid down without saying anything and with his back to me.

"Jahfar, nothing happened," I said, trying to reassure him.

"Fuck you, Misty," he said, and I was done trying to convince him. I wondered if Kayla was going through the same shit that I was on the other side of town.

Kayla Gambino

I couldn't believe that Misty and I had gotten caught so damn quickly. The moment I walked into the house I was being questioned like a mad man. Fu wouldn't stop until I finally told him my whereabouts, but the moment I opened my mouth I was caught. I said we had gone to the nail spa and my brother told him we went to lunch and a movie. Shit was just crazy and once I uttered the words abortion out of my mouth, it was like I saw the human form of rage.

Fu was so mad that he berated me like a child and then proceeded to tear my house up. Every picture that hung the walls was now resting on the floor. I didn't know that he would be this angry, to the point that he scared me. I mean, I expected him to be upset but that person he became last night was a person that I would never want to cross.

I got up from my dining room chair overlooking my fucked-up ass house. The fact that I would have to clean all of this shit up made me tired already. It wasn't until I heard the horn honking outside that I realized that Game was coming to get me for lunch. Usually, we would discuss the monthly sales for the K-Spot, but somehow, I knew that this lunch would be different.

THE REALEST IN THE GAME WANTS HER

I got into the car and Nipsey Hussle's "Grinding All My Life" was blasting through the speakers. I swear he was going to wear this damn album out. He finally turned down the music and just shook his head at me.

"Don't start Jahfar. I'm not in the mood today," I said, hoping that he would leave me the fuck alone with his piercing stare.

"I don't care what you're in the mood for. You're dirty, yo." He continued to shake his head.

"Okay, well let me be dirty then."

"Why you kill that man baby Kay? That shit was selfish as hell."

"I'm not about to sit here and defend my actions to you. It was my body and my choice."

"But that was his baby too Kay. Damn, the least you could have done was talk to the nigga about it," he preached.

"For what? So, he could try and talk me out of it? With everything that happened with him and Danni, I just wasn't ready to have his baby."

"Man, it's really not even my business so I'ma leave it alone."

"Yeah, fine time to mind your business. And anyway, why you all up in my Kool-Aid when you got your own problems in your back yard?"

"Fuck you talking about girl?"

I turned and faced him. "Uhh, you and Misty. You snapped on her for nothing at all. That girl didn't do nothing wrong."

"No, y'all was on some hoe shit getting numbers at Walmart. I've been embarrassed in a relationship before and it won't happen again."

"Well maybe if you would've listened to her and believed her, you wouldn't have embarrassed your damn self. You know I'm not gone lie for her. I put that damn number in her phone after he paid for MY stuff. She wouldn't even look at his ass out of respect for yo' ass."

I was getting hot at his stubborn self.

"Oh, and another thing, you have a beautiful girlfriend. She literally turns heads when we are out. If you don't want niggas stepping to her, she's not the one for you. Be lucky she shuts shit down and is not a slimy slut like your BM."

"Man, watch yo' mouth."

"You just make sure you make things right with my girl because with or without you, she's still gone be my sis."

The rest of the car ride was silent, and I knew that my brother was in deep thought. Now I just had to get my relationship right while I was all in his.

Fuquan Grimes

The first time I was ever close to knocking a bitch's head off was when Kayla told me that she killed my seed. The funny thing was, I would've taken care of the baby by myself if I had to. I was cool on Kayla for a lil' minute, so now I was back at my baby mama's crib kicking it with my baby. My baby was four years old and easily the best thing that ever happened to me.

Her mama and I couldn't stand each other. I asked her to get an abortion because honestly, Chi Chi and I were just fuck buddies and had been since I was fifteen. Chi was just a good time, but she wasn't shit for real. No ambition, no goals, no drive, no nothing. Just good pussy. I knew that I shouldn't have been here, but Kayla had done something to me that I couldn't let go. The first girl that I ever loved had betrayed me and didn't even have a real answer as to why. Kayla was the youngest out of the crew until her brother came along, so of course, she was spoiled as hell, but I didn't expect her to be this damn selfish.

"Da Da, let's play doll babies," my daughter, Isis, said holding up these jacked-up ass dolls, hair missing and everything.

"Okay baby, but do I have to be a girl doll?" I asked, serious as hell.

She always had me being this doll that she named Jamari. Where she got that name, I don't know.

"Yes Daddy. You are Jamari, remember?"

"Okay baby. Hey girl," I said, making my voice high-pitched to sound like a girl. My baby just fell back laughing. She loved my girl voice. Just as we started our game, her mama walked in and I knew that it was time for me to go now.

I picked my daughter up and kissed her forehead goodbye.

"You don't have to leave 'cause I'm here," she said while twisting by. It was a regular ass day and she was wearing some bullshit.

"You not cold man? It's March and you out here walking around like it's the summertime or something."

She only smirked at me and went twisting into the kitchen, her ass poking in the coochie cutter pants that she was wearing. Shit had big ass holes all through them.

"Isis, go on upstairs for a minute. I have to talk to your daddy!" she yelled.

"Do I have to Daddy?" she asked while pouting.

"Yeah, baby girl. Go to your room for just a minute and I will come before I leave."

She ran her little feet up to her room and there stood Chi just staring at me.

"What's up Chiara? And don't ask me for shit because I just put $1000 in your account last week."

"Dang, baby daddy. Why you always got to think I want something from you?" She walked closer to me and had the nerve to try and kiss me. As many dicks as she sucked, I wouldn't even let her kiss my dog. All the niggas in the hood knew that my baby mama was a certified

THE REALEST IN THE GAME WANTS HER

freak and if it wasn't for my street credibility, I would've been the laughing stock of the town.

"Yo, what I tell you about that shit?" I snapped.

"I'm sorry baby," she said in a childlike voice. It was the same voice she used when she wanted some shit.

"I got something you can put your mouth around though."

She smiled as if she had just won the lottery and instantly dropped to her knees before getting up again and flying out. She came right back out with cut up pieces of grapefruit.

"What you about to do with that shit?" I had never experimented with grapefruit before.

"You will see," she said seductively before she put the grapefruit around my dick and went crazy. She didn't even start off slow, but instead, she went full throttle moving the grapefruit up and down my dick while she sucked the skin off my shit. I didn't want to howl out like a lil' bitch, but she was making the shit hard as hell. My daughter was upstairs and shit so I definitely had to calm the fuck down. I looked down and her pretty little head and she went down to my balls, swallowing them whole. The next thing she did really caught me off guard.

As she stroked my dick, she eased her pinky in my butt. My fucking asshole! I hit her damn head so hard that she flew across the room.

"Why did you do that?!" she yelled as if she hadn't just tried me on some gay shit.

"Bitch, fuck type of niggas you been fucking with that like you to play in their ass? You got me fucked up."

"Boy, calm yo' ass down. Ain't nothing wrong with a little anal play," she said, getting up like it was nothing.

"Bitch, this will be the last time that you ever come close to my dick again. Nasty bitch!"

"Whatever nigga, carry your bitch ass back home to the basic bitch you're with now."

I walked up to her and she backed up, knowing that she was playing a dangerous game.

"Yeah, now yo' ass scared. Stop fucking playing with me man. Shut the fuck up when I'm talking and don't ever mention my girl again." I didn't even have to touch her for her to feel me.

I went up to kiss my baby goodnight and left her nasty ass mama shaking. This would be my last time acting off my weak ass emotions. That shit only got you in trouble.

Misty Blue

I had to put my damn seatbelt on messing with Kayla. She was driving like a bat out of hell and talking a mile a minute.

"This nigga got me bent. We haven't even been broken up for forty-eight hours and now he's back dipping with his baby mother."

I couldn't even get a word in. She just went on and on with her rant.

"He thinks I'm stupid. He probably was still fucking with her the whole time!"

"How do you even know he's there Kay?" I asked

"Because you know the bitch still stay in the hood and the hood got eyes everywhere. I'm going to kill him just like I did his dead ass baby."

"Oh my god Kayla, why did you have to drag me along? I have my own shit to deal with."

I hadn't spoken to Game and he didn't even try to call. He was in his own world and blaming me for shit that I didn't do. Men were just dumb sometimes and I wasn't going to be the next dumb chick to chase after him. I did miss him though; the way he called my last name even though I hated it, and the way he made me feel like I had family because I didn't have my parents. Oh, and then there was that Vitamin D that he blessed me with daily. I missed the hell out of that too.

We made it to Fu's baby mama's house just as he was walking out, and the look on his face let us know that he wasn't for any bull. But Kayla didn't care as she didn't waste any time going in.

"The fuck are you doing here Fuquan? You were that mad at me that you ran back to the hood with your baby mama?"

"Man, calm yo' slow ass down. Did you forget that my daughter lives here too? I came to see my damn baby."

"Well, Fu, how long do you have to spend with your daughter here? Somebody said you was up in that bitch for damn near four hours. You couldn't take her to Chuck E Cheese or something?"

"Man, I can be in there for however the fuck long I want to. I'm not dealing with your dumb ass today." He tried walking past her, but she stopped him.

"Don't walk away from me while I'm standing here talking to you Fuquan," she snapped. By now, people started to stop and stare.

"Fuck are you doing Kayla? You came out here to give these people a show or something? Go the fuck home before you piss me off."

She piped down a little, but I could tell that she was visibly upset, and he was too. I was about to chime in until I heard someone yell out Game's name.

"LOORRRDDDD!" I said out loud, and everyone looked at me like I was crazy. It was so crazy that I could even smell his scent before he reached me, and once again, everyone flocked to him like he was P Diddy or somebody. It was honestly annoying.

"Welp Kay, I can see that you're going to leave with Fu tonight so I'm going to take your car and go."

THE REALEST IN THE GAME WANTS HER

"She's not going with me," Fu said, looking at me like I was crazy. Kayla only rolled her eyes at him.

"Girl, we are about to go TOGETHER," she said, dragging out together.

"Yeah, take yo' crazy ass home," Fu co-signed.

"Where you going?" I didn't even see Game sneaking up on me. I just kept walking while he followed.

"You don't hear me talking to you Blue?" he asked again.

"Yes, and I am ignoring you."

"Why you want to do that?" he asked as if I was mad by myself. Just two days ago, he wouldn't even speak to me.

"Jahfar, leave me alone. I've been hurt too many times in my life, and I won't let it happen again. Just leave me be."

"Nah, I can't do that."

"Okay, well talk to yourself."

I was steadily walking and by now, I had passed the car so mad and confused about what I was feeling for him.

"We can do this all night. You're not leaving until you talk to me."

"What do you want Jahfar? DAMN!" I finally stopped walking and faced him.

"You're so pretty when you're are mad," he said smiling, but I didn't find him funny. He was playing with me.

"And you are ugly," I replied.

He chuckled slightly. "You're wild man."

"No, you are wild man," I mocked.

He laughed. "Why are you acting like you so tough? Huh? You don't miss your man?"

"Uhhh, you haven't given me time to miss you."

"Well I miss you, so let's make up. How you gone act?" He stood there with his nonchalant stature and I hated it.

"How you gone act does not sound like an apology. You think you're funny, but you really hurt my feelings accusing me of things that I didn't do. You're always pinning things on me, so how about I go and do something for real?"

Now his Mike Epps acting self wasn't laughing. He just stood there with his arms folded, looking down at me.

"You're right, I shouldn't have accused you, so my bad for that. You know that I would never hurt you. You just have to let your guard down a little bit."

"ANNDDD."

"And what, Blue? Damn!!"

Now I was laughing. "For kicking me out of YOUR house."

"Man, I didn't kick you out."

"Yeah, but you also didn't make me feel like I could stay after the argument. But now I have my own, so you won't have to ever worry about that again." I shook my keys in his face.

"You're a shit talker yo, but are we good?" He grabbed me tightly for an embrace while passersby stared with envy. I even heard a couple of girls gawk.

"There goes your fan club," I commented, and he only smirked.

"Well if it ain't my little brother?" I heard a voice approaching us, and it was Jaylen. Hopefully these two could behave tonight. He spoke to me and I waved because Game was giving me the death stare. There was also a guy walking up behind him, and the closer he got, I got a little nervous because he looked so familiar.

"What are you doing around these parts brother?" Jaylen asked with a sly grin. "I thought you forgot about where you came from."

"Nah, I didn't forget where I came from, but I had sense enough to get out," Game responded callously.

"Big man, big man. It must feel like a king to be you," Jaylen said. His voice reeked of venom.

His friend that walked up kept staring at me, but I only looked away.

"You got something you want to say to me Jaylen? This small talk isn't necessary."

"Oh, you want me to talk in front of your girl, Miss Misty Blue?" The way he said my name sent chills through my spine, and not in a good way.

Game grilled him like he wanted to say more, but he only kept quiet, which was the first time that I had ever witnessed him backing down from his brother.

"I think pay day is going to come a little early this month," Jaylen said to his friend, and they both laughed. I was trying to read between the lines because there was seriously something weird going on that I was clearly not in on.

The two then walked off and on the way, Jaylen's friend looked back.

"Bye Misty," he said and then blew me a kiss.

I cringed as I knew what was about to happen. Before I could even protest, Game hawked him down and was on top of him hitting him with the butt of his gun. Everyone who was outside dispersed like there was a certain street code that they abided by. If no one saw anything, they wouldn't know anything. Blood leaked into the concrete and I couldn't take any more so I ran to the car, only for Game to join me five minutes later. I didn't know if the guy was dead or what from the way that Game had decorated his face.

The ride back to his house was silent and when we finally got in, I wanted to say something to him, but I was honestly scared. He walked over and reached out to me and I jumped.

"Don't touch me," I mumbled.

I didn't get why he had to go that far tonight all because someone had spoken to me. After only remembering bits and pieces of my mother dying, but knowing that it was violent, seeing Game so enraged made me start to see a different side to him that I didn't like.

"Bae, I know you've never seen me act like that before, but I promise you don't have to be scared of me," he said lovingly, but he still put fear in me.

"Why did you have to do all of that?" I asked sadly.

He gently grabbed me and sat me down on the bed.

"Bae, I told you I'm big on respect. It's always one person who tries it, so I had to let him know. The nigga was disrespectful like he knew you or something."

My stomach was now in knots as I debated if I should just come clean or go on quietly. I knew Game despised liars though, and I didn't want him to think that he couldn't trust me.

"Well, I don't know him, but I've seen him before. He was the guy who paid for our things in Walmart."

"The nigga whose number was in your phone?"

"Yeah."

"Small ass world that one of my biggest enemies would be the one you meet at Walmart."

"Right, and it's an even smaller world that one of your biggest enemies is all chummy with your brother. What was all that that pay day stuff he was talking about tonight?"

"Nothing that you need to worry your pretty ass about." He kissed my forehead and then we hopped into the shower. I knew that there was more to the story than he was telling me, but I would not probe. The truth would eventually reveal itself.

Fuquan Grimes

When I say that my head was banging from all the shit that had gone down today. Yeah, I was still pissed at Kayla, but I also felt bad that I was on some fuck shit and went to see my baby mama. I'm glad her ass didn't come outside with her bullshit when Kayla came. That shit saved my ass.

I planned on being mad at Kayla a little longer, but to be honest, I couldn't stay away from her for too long. She was turning me into a sucka ass nigga for real, and though the trust still wasn't fully there, I couldn't deny the love that I had for her.

I finished up my shower and planned to get some ass and be knocked out after. Kayla was gone be hanging from chandeliers tonight fucking with me. She had a whole bunch of fucking and sucking to do to be back in my good graces completely.

I walked out of the fogged-up bathroom and Kayla was sitting on the bed; just sitting and looking, not doing anything. Both of our phones were sitting beside her and I didn't even care if she went through my shit 'cause wasn't anything in there.

THE REALEST IN THE GAME WANTS HER

"You're still doing dumb shit, I see," I said, and she only smiled, but it was a weird smile.

"I don't know if it was the death of my nephew or what, but she has clearly lost her damn mind," she said calmly.

"Hell she do now?" I asked, knowing she was talking about Danni.

"She's still texting your phone, and she had a lot more to say this time."

"I'm not even worried about that shit," I said, waving her off.

Fu, you can act like that one night didn't mean anything to you, but it meant everything to me. I don't care if it was only one time, that doesn't change the fact that it happened. Yeah, it was before you and Kay, but it happened. After I had my son, I was vulnerable because my baby daddy wasn't doing right, and you being one of my best friends came to comfort me, but that comfort turned into a little more and I just think that we should tell my sister. Whatever y'all want to do after is up to y'all, but she needs to know. She read the text out.

All I could do was shake my head.

"Ma, it was way before you," I stated.

"It doesn't matter if it was before me Fuquan. You had sex with my sister and me, and I didn't know about it. The whole time I'm thinking she's just tripping, but it was because you were on some foul shit. You shouldn't have even approached me knowing that you and my sister had relations before, no matter how miniscule you thought it was. You know half of me needed to hear you say that she was lying, but she wasn't so you couldn't."

"Kayla, I don't want to minimize how you feel right now and yeah, I should've been upfront with you, but that shit happened years ago, and it was barely a fuck."

She walked up to me and mushed the fuck out of my face. "No one told you to fuck that girl and now you think I'm just supposed to let it fly because it was a long time ago? Do you know how dirty I feel? You and I are done!"

"Kayla, choose your words wisely," I said. "If you say we're done, ain't no coming back from it. We've both kept shit from one another, but I didn't just give up on you."

"Fuquan, fuck that bastard ass baby that you keep bringing up. Glad I didn't keep the shit," she spat, really trying to hurt me. "Now, get out!" she yelled.

For real, I was tired of arguing with her, so I didn't even put up a fight. If she wanted to end us over this dumb shit, then so be it. I walked out, signaling the end of our relationship.

Misty Blue

I was shocked to say the least when I got a call from Ava saying that she needed me to pick her up and not to tell her dad. At first, I was thinking it was a set up, but the urgency and fear in her voice let me know that something was really wrong. I left the library in a hurry and thanked God that today I was driving one of Game's cars. She shot me her location and I was there within ten minutes.

It looked like some type of party was going on and there were kids posted up outside and on the porch of a townhouse. I didn't even have to go in because Ava came running out, and she looked distraught as hell. She ran straight into my arms and my mind automatically went to a dark place.

"Ava! Are you okay? What happened? Did someone hurt you?" I asked, while she held on to my waist so tight that it was becoming difficult for me to breathe.

"Nothing happened. Can we just go home?"

Without saying anything, I walked her to the car and as I drove, we were both silent.

"Sweetie, you're going to have to tell me something. Your father will know that something is wrong with you and I won't be able to back you up if I don't know what's going on."

"It's really stupid," she said while wiping her falling tears. "So, there was this boy that I liked, and I was supposed to meet him here tonight. My dad actually thinks that I'm at a friend's sleepover right now, but we snuck to this party. So, when I got there, I went in the bedroom to put my coat up, when I saw the boy that I liked and my other friend kissing. I don't know what else happened, but her pants were down, and I just ran out."

I held my chest, so happy that what I thought happened, didn't. I for sure thought some little boy had tried something with her, and though Ava was butt hurt, she would be fine. This teen drama would be over before she knew it. I couldn't imagine her going through anything remotely close to the things that I had been through being so young.

"Aww Ava, I'm so sorry. I know it hurts, but everything will be okay. This just showed you who your real friends are." I patted her back.

"Right. I can't believe I let her borrow my Gucci bag and everything."

I laughed because why in the hell does her thirteen-year-old ass even have a Gucci bag when I was still rocking Guess?

"Now, I'm not going to tell your dad, but you have to promise me that you won't sneak out like this again. Anything could've happened to you."

"I promise I won't. And thank you for coming to get me." She grabbed my hand and held it for the entire ride home.

Good thing Game was still out when we got home so we slid into our pjs and rented movies. If he was to ask why she was home, we would say that she started feeling sick and wanted to come home. That night Ava and I kicked it like we were old friends. This was the first time that I had gotten more than five words out of her. I didn't know if I was tripping , but something about her was so familiar to me. All in all, I was just happy that she was finally giving me a chance. Too bad the harmony wouldn't last.

* * *

1 week later

I was low-key panicking inside. I had a special night planned for Game and I, and I wanted everything to go off without a hitch. To me, it was more than a dinner to show my appreciation to him, but more so, a dinner where we could be our very best, true selves.

I was running a little behind because I had been held up at the beauty salon for hours. I never understood why you would schedule an appointment for one time but wouldn't make it to the stylist's chair until hours later. Finally done up, I had to meet the caterers at Game's house so they could place the food. Kayla was doing me a favor by keeping Game busy all day, so as far as I knew he didn't suspect a thing.

I made it home to let the caterers in and showered and put on a form-fitting slip dress. My soft curls bounced with every step that I took, and I knew that Game would be eating his heart out tonight. I checked the food and everything looked great, but I strongly doubted that he would do very much eating tonight. The whole little set up looked perfect and now I was just waiting for the guest of honor to arrive.

The door opening made me a little nervous, but it was now or never. I grabbed the champagne flute from the table and filled it with Rozay. I met Game at the door with his glass and he looked surprised out of his mind.

"Bae, what is all of this?" he asked, smiling like a kid when he saw the entire spread.

"It's all for you babe. I don't think we've had much us time lately, so I wanted to do something for us. Now sit." I led him to the table, piled his plate with food and gave it to him.

"Damn right! Serve your man!" he said, smacking my booty, causing it to jiggle. I planted a delicate yet intense kiss on his lips which I thought of as the kiss of death. Some bullshit ass music played in the back and the lights were dimmed giving the night an enchanted kind of look.

Game went in on his food like I knew his big ass would.

"Babe, we were supposed to do this before we started eating, but let's make a toast." I raised my glass to his.

"What are we toasting to?"

"Umm, let's toast to coming out." I smiled.

"Coming out? What you mean? Everyone already knows we're together."

"No silly. Coming out, like all of our truths and lies coming out."

He looked at me with a weird look on his face. I could tell the shit that I put in his drink was starting to take effect. His eyes became a little glossy and his words slurred while I just smiled.

"Fuuhhh, fuuuckk you do to me?" he finally got out.

"Ohhh, I spiked your drink. You will be knocked out in a few seconds, so don't even try anything stupid."

No sooner than those words left my mouth, his head dropped on the table. So far, everything was going just perfectly. I looked perfect, and my plan was perfect so tonight would be perfect.

I raced up the stairs, not wasting any time because Game's spiked drink would wear off in about an hour. My first stop was to his safe. I watched him put his code in so many times that I had the shit memorized. There sat several stacks of money to go with the money that I had already cleaned from his bank account. Game trusted me so much that he wasn't even careful when leaving his bank statements and shit lying around. This man had close to ten million in the bank. Well, now I had close to ten million.

Next, I grabbed my suitcase that I hid under the bed along with my plane tickets and loaded everything in the car. I changed out of my fancy ass dress and put on a sweat suit. Still, everything was going perfectly and now I just had to finish the deed. About forty-five minutes had passed and I was sitting coolly waiting for sleeping beauty to awake.

A few minutes later, he slowly started to lift his head and the first thing he did was try to make a run for it, but that wasn't happening due to the fact that he was handcuffed to the radiator.

"Fuck is going on Misty? Get me out of these fucking handcuffs now!" he shouted assertively when he realized that he wasn't dreaming but was about to experience his worst nightmare.

"Fuck is going on Misty?" I mocked him. "You don't know?" I said, waving the loaded gun that I had in my hands to show him that there were no games being played tonight. I looked the devil straight in his eyes never expecting for him to show an ounce of fear because he was never scared and even if he was, he would never show it.

"No, I don't know! And I really don't give a fuck," he said, trying to snatch the cuffs from the radiator, but he only ended up hurting himself.

"Ha-ha, that's what your ass gets. But enough stalling," I said, looking at my watch. "I have a flight to catch in two hours and I can't be late. What haunts you at night? I see you tossing and turning."

His eyes became cold and I knew he knew exactly what I was getting to.

"Your whole life you've tried to be the good guy, righting your wrongs. So again, what haunts you nigga?" I yelled, letting off a shot, hitting his leg. He was taking too long and frankly, I was getting bored.

"Ahhh shit!" he yelled out in agony. "Misty, put the fucking gun down!"

"Don't tell me what to do! You thought I didn't know BITCH? Those masks shielded your faces, but not your souls. It took me a few years to figure out that it was you and your buffoon ass cousin who did that to me that night! All the good shit that you've decided to do in your life doesn't matter now because that shit won't bring my parents back. NONE OF IT!"

His head dropped and I walked over to him and butted him with the gun. The blood easing from his head reminded me of the red hots that we used to get on Valentine's Day.

"Nigga, look up when I'm talking to you." I rushed over and yanked him by his face. "Don't try to feel sorry for yourself now. My father let you and your sleezy cousin into our house and that's how you repay him?? Huh?? You rape his daughter and kill his wife? Did you know that after you beat her, you made her have a heart attack. She couldn't take what you were doing to her and her heart exploded, you pig!" I yelled, kicking him in his side.

"Misty, I promise I didn't do any of that. I could've, no, I should've done more to help y'all, but I didn't touch either of you, and I cut Rod off after that!" he roared with so much empathy in his voice that I almost believed him. Too bad I wasn't that little naïve girl anymore.

"Nope. You won't do this to me again. Stop trying to make me believe your lying ass. It's that type of shit that almost made me forget my mission in the first place. From the moment I saw you at your sister's spot, I knew it was you. I searched for you for years, but you went under the radar and when I finally found you, I debated what I wanted to do with your ass or if you were even worth my time. So, when you started being all nice to me, the opportunity presented itself, and I went for it.

"THEN!!!" I shouted, startling him. "You made me fall in love with you. I went into the situation having one motive, and that was to

THE REALEST IN THE GAME WANTS HER

avenge my mother's death, but you made me love you so much that I had even forgiven you. I fucking forgave you! I actually fell in love with the man who took my family away from me. STUPID ME!" I used the gun to scratch my head while the tears poured from my eyes.

"You want to know when all that changed?" I asked, looking him dead in his face. "ANSWER ME DAMMIT!" I let a shot go off in the air.

Game only looked at me with stone-cold eyes.

"The night your weak ass brother challenged you. At first, I didn't know what the fuck was going on, but I figured out that you were paying him to keep quiet. He knew what you and your jailbird cousin did, and he was blackmailing you. But instead of you being a man about it and owning what you did, you continued paying him year after year. You thought you were so slick hitting me with all that shit about how y'all didn't get along because he was jealous of you, when in all reality, he had a one up on your dirty ass. You paid him like what you did to my mother could be erased with your hush money! That night, I knew you hadn't changed at all."

"Misty, you NEED to believe me. I never meant to hurt you or your family. A piece of me died that night too. Shit wasn't supposed to go down like that!"

"Then how was it supposed to go down? Y'all would just rob us and ride off to the fucking sunset? Y'all took more than money from us that night and because of you, I went through hell growing up. I feared everything, so I isolated myself from the world. And the only man that ever loved me left me. My daddy couldn't take looking in my face every day knowing that I reminded him so much of my mom, so he left," I said sadly.

"If I could take it all back, I would. He isn't the only person who loves you. I love you," he started, but I was tired of hearing his bullshit lies.

POP went the sound of the bullet that I sent crashing through his other leg.

"Ahhhh fuck!" he screamed, but he refused to give me more than that. He was sweating bullets and I knew that he was in pain, no matter how he tried to hide it.

"Misty, you can do what the fuck you want to me now, but if there is any way that I can get out of this shit, I will hurt you. You're not about to take me away from my girls."

The irony of his statement made me chuckle.

"Fuck those little bitches." I quickly wiped the sweat from my forehead.

"I should kill them too, but I want them to feel the same hurt and pain that I felt. You better be lucky that I will leave their mom to raise them. You took both of my parents from me."

"Misty, no matter how hard you try to fight those feelings in your heart, you know you love me."

"Shut up!" I said emotionlessly. "Love doesn't live here anymore." I raised the gun to his head and he looked at me fearlessly.

"Waiiittt! No, please don't, MOM!" I heard a voice say from behind me. I turned around to see Ava standing there shaking like a leaf. I turned back to Game and he just shook his head.

"I'm your daughter, Misty," she said lowly. "I never said anything, but when I did the ancestry and genogram thing in school a few weeks back, I learned that my DNA didn't match my mom's or my dad's. One day while I was snooping through my dad's things, I saw a birth certificate that listed you as my birth mother," she said all in one voice.

I was really losing it at this point and from the look in Game's eyes, I could tell he had more to say.

"She's not lying Misty. After the shit went down with your family, I never saw you again up until about eight months later. I was in the hospital with Danni after she had a false alarm with her first baby when I saw some people bringing you in. I didn't even know that you were pregnant, so imagine my surprise when I saw you panting while holding your belly. I waited it out and found your room about three hours later. You were knocked out, so I know you don't remember, but I saw the adoption papers lying beside you. Like you said, me trying to right my wrongs, I stalked your baby until I turned eighteen and could adopt her. By now, she was already placed with a family, but money talked. I adopted her and Bregan and I raised her as our own. She was too little to remember, so she fit right in with us and I never treated her any differently from Logan," he spat out.

I couldn't believe that this shit was happening. I had never told a soul that I gave my kid up after becoming pregnant after I was raped by Rod. I was ashamed and I knew that at twelve years old, I couldn't raise a child. Now, here she was being raised by Game the entire time, and the shit just further enraged me. Like, how long did he think that he would be able to hide this shit from me? Did he think that we would just be together and I wouldn't start to ask any questions? I always questioned in my head how he had a daughter so old in age, but I never minded it. Nigga was slower than I thought.

What kind of fucking game was he playing? He had really gone and got my kid and played daddy to her. I sank down to the floor and sobbed to myself, and Ava, my daughter, came and hugged me. I wanted to push her away, but I hugged her closer. She smelled like me, and she even felt like me. Being wrapped in her warmth felt so damn good, but now I was conflicted. I didn't know whether I should finish what I sought out to do or if I should run and hide. I had been gamed and I didn't know what to do.

Who will win in this game of love and war. . .

To be continued.

ABOUT THE AUTHOR

Teshera Cooper is a 27-year-old new author who hails from Norfolk, Virginia. She has a bachelor's degree in psychology from Old Dominion University. While she has a passion for mental health and advocates for black excellence that has never stopped her from turning the vivid imagery that consumes her thoughts into short stories. She has been writing short stories since about 14 years old and drew inspiration from her upbringing and from her experiences from growing up in the "hood". Each of the characters that she creates embodies someone that she has encountered; from the dope boys on the street corner to the hot in the pants girl who deep down inside just wants to be loved.

Teshera is devoted to giving her readers a fast paced and gritty thrill ride with a twist of hood love. Writers who have inspired her include, Terri woods, Sista Soulja, Carl Webber, Wahida Clark, Vickie Stranger, K'wan, Ashley & Jaquavis and countless others. The way that they can bring life into their characters with just the stroke of a pen is pure genius and that is what she aspires to do through her writing.

facebook.com/TeelaMarieCooper

instagram.com/Teela_marie18

Royalty Publishing House is now accepting manuscripts from aspiring or experienced urban romance authors!

WHAT MAY PLACE YOU ABOVE THE REST:

Heroes who are the ultimate book bae: strong-willed, maybe a little rough around the edges but willing to risk it all for the woman he loves.

Heroines who are the ultimate match: the girl next door type, not perfect - has her faults but is still a decent person. One who is willing to risk it all for the man she loves.

The rest is up to you! Just be creative, think out of the box, keep it sexy and intriguing!

If you'd like to join the Royal family, send us the first 15K words (60 pages) of your completed manuscript to submissions@royaltypublishinghouse.com

LIKE OUR PAGE!

ROYALTY
PUBLISHING HOUSE

Be sure to LIKE our Royalty Publishing House page on Facebook!

CPSIA information can be obtained
at www.ICGtesting.com
Printed in the USA
LVHW111627071119
636673LV00005B/954/P

9 781703 043310